POCKET MONEY

BY

M F LAMPHERE

Pocket Money
By M F Lamphere
Copyright © 2016 M F Lamphere

ISBN-13: 978-1530732647
ISBN-10: 1530732646

Cover Design by M F Lamphere

POCKET MONEY

BY

M F LAMPHERE

This book is dedicated to every writer who thinks they can.
This book is proof that you are correct.

May 22, 1992

9:50 a.m.

I hate this day.

I had an 8 a.m. final, my last of the semester, my last as an undergrad. The latter points are cool, but 8 a.m.? What sadistic psychopath scheduled that? Oh, that's right, the Dean of the Psychology department. I'm sure we were test subjects in a thesis study or guinea pigs in some behavioral perspective experiment. *Let's see how the content validity of early morning students compares against afternoon students given identical environments and similar exams, blah, blah, blah.*

Fuck 'em. I'm pretty sure I blew their curve, hope I was in the control.

Four years I played the university game. Attended the classes, took the tests, ran the studies. Eight semesters and what do I have to show for it? The opportunity to go to more school, for more years. I have no idea what I'm going to do when I finish. I just know I have to keep going—there are no job opportunities for undergrad psych degrees. Well, there are, but all the high school kids are working them.

I roll my shoulders and stretch, pressing my palms against the ceiling of the car while controlling the steering wheel with one knee. After the hellacious couple of days I just had, my body is rebelling. My eyes lead the coup by closing and I blink rapidly before forcing them open. *Stay,* I command.

The drive-thru coffee I picked up on my way out of town has yet to give me a caffeine boost. I should've just gotten a Coke at McDonald's, saved myself four bucks on the useless splurge and guaranteed a reliable buzz. I take a deep drag on the cigarette and grimace at the taste. Not my brand.

Yawning, I roll down the window, hoping the morning air will help. The sun burns too bright, too early—in the day and the season. A hot, muggy gust rips into the car. I flick the generous butt out the opening and crank the handle in reverse.

My fingertips rub through patchy scruff, feeling a week's worth of growth on my baby-faced cheeks and chin. This is about as good as it gets. After much razor-avoidance, I'm the proud bearer of a three o'clock shadow.

I smack my face in an effort to energize. The burst of physical adrenaline perks me up. Unsatisfying, but it gets the job done. I pop in the cassette for *The Commitments* soundtrack to keep me there.

I'm on my way home. *Home?* I think, and struggle to find a better term. After nearly four years away, "home" seems like a stretch. It is where my mother lives, though. I hope it's nice to see her.

My car is loaded with everything I own, which despite the blocked view through the rear view mirror, is not much. The essentials, really. Clothes, bedding, and personal shit.

Too poor to be wasteful, I tossed my half empty toiletries in my Scooby Doo garbage can. Even took the leftover roll of toilet paper. Sorry apartment cleaners and painters, take it up with the management. Four years of life living on my own are packed into my Mercury Lynx hatchback, just one more temporary home for my crap until I move to grad school in August.

In the meantime, I'll be sleeping on the floor of my mom's place. She has a studio apartment in the pre-gentrified Art District of town. "Investment property," she says, as if she'll be grandfathered into rent control once they complete the turnover. As if she's ever stayed anywhere that long. I haven't seen it yet, but for what she says she pays, I imagine it's no bigger than this car.

I glance over my shoulder and grin. The "halo" is propped up between a crammed duffle bag, a plastic milk crate full of books and the laundry basket. The giant letter "O" is wrapped haphazardly in a Mystery Machine comforter. As you may have guessed, I have a soft spot for Scooby and Friends.

Traffic is crawling and it pisses me off, construction season has begun. I slam on my horn and brakes in tandem as some dickhead who waited 'til the last possible moment to zip into the one remaining lane cuts me off. Would've been effortless to crash into him. *Murder*, I think, *some days it seems so easy.*

The road opens again and I crank the volume, singing loudly about Sally slowing that Mustang down as I gun it, maneuvering my car onto the highway.

Driving with a lead foot and heavy head, I wonder why I am doing this. Despite the Bachelor of Science that I have just earned in Psychology, my BS degree—how apropos—I am no smarter than when I left. How else do you explain returning oneself willingly to an environment you fought so hard to escape.

Because it *is* home.

11:47 a.m.

It's funny, I probably drove this road more as a high schooler heading out to parties than I have since I moved away to college. Four years and I could count on two hands how many times I've come back.

Maybe if my mom hadn't relocated between practically every visit, I'd have been more inclined to come and stay. I always made time for Christmas, but that's about it.

Clicking the indicator, I swerve around some under-the-speed-limit-more-likely-than-a-speeder-to-cause-an-accident asshole and wonder if my mom still has her "holiday" tree up. Probably. It's a bunch of long branches she found, and by "found" I mean she mutilated a couple of not quite dead trees at the park to give their limbs a second incarnation.

Stripping the branches bare, she painted them white and stuck the cluster in one of those old glass carboys. She hangs crap off of it all year 'round. Colored eggs and flowers, candy with black and orange streamers, glass icicles and antique ornaments. I'll admit, I'm kind of curious to see what celebration May conjures.

Fuck, why'd I think that? May conjures pain.

I can't even summon a smirk at the vision of stark branches adorned with tiny Cabbage Patch Doll clothes, wild-haired Trolls hanging heavy on slender rods, or My Little Ponies straddling white twigs.

I shudder and take in a mouthful of cold coffee. The sensory revulsion snaps me out of this dreadful chain of thoughts.

As if in reaction to my agonizing emotions, *Chain of Fools* comes up on random. I jab the button and switch tracks. We're all weak links in somebody's chain, no need for further reminders.

Up ahead are the signs for the turn-offs. Wow, that went fast. I don't even remember merging onto this road. Despite my infrequent visits, my autopilot seems to work just fine.

My hometown is not big by any means, but there's a university that doubles the population nine months of the year. They let out last week. I'm not actually from here, but here is the longest place I've ever lived.

The city is large enough, spread out enough, to warrant three highway exits. I speed past the first ramp, the one that would take me to where my mother currently resides, and instead merge onto the second option.

The toll is higher here, I always forget that. I'm at a dead stop for as long as it takes me to scrounge up sixty-five cents. Grabbing fistfuls of pennies from the ashtray, I toss them in the basket until the gate lifts. I miss the days of manned booths where a quarter and a little sweet talk or a friendly high-five could get you through.

I can't believe I'm going to meet up with these guys. Old friends I left behind when I graduated high school. *Escaped, remember.*

But Rick had called, said he ran into my mom who told him I'd be moving back today and gave him my number. He was his charming old persuasive self and then Freddy called and made me "an offer I couldn't refuse," and they both promised that Stoney would be there, too, and well, I kind of miss Stoney.

I skip through a couple of tracks on the cassette before eventually switching the stereo over to the radio. The chorus from *Ghost in You* by the Psychedelic Furs caresses my ears and I turn it up, crooning around a broad smile.

Junior year we dubbed ourselves the Psychedelic Fours for the homecoming talent show. We dressed in drag and sang *Pretty in Pink*, dedicating it to our foes, the Hyland Maroons.

What kind of mascot is a Maroon? All these years later, I still don't know.

We were pretty toasted that night. I don't think anybody was far enough gone to think we were actually good, but I know it took an extra helping of the bud to get me on stage in a dress.

Yellow stripes and reflective signs shout "slow down" in the elementary school zone and I comply as I envy the new playground equipment. Bold colors and smooth plastics have replaced the worn metal we enjoyed as preteens.

I chuckle to myself as I see my friends and I take turns with Rick's fat skateboard down the middle of the steep silver slide. Freddy earned nine stitches that day, cracking the back of head on the edge. He'd almost made it. I rub my shoulder and think about the sling I earned slamming into the steel rail trying to catch him.

Accelerating past the brand new drug store, a chain that's popping up at every other intersection, I am filled with melancholy at what I fear is the loss of small town America. The 'Grand Opening' banners can't blot out the vision of Garrett's Drug & Ice Cream Shoppe. As I pass the corner, I see the four of us, maybe fifteen years old, sucking on filters of whatever cigarettes Rick had pilfered while we distracted the counter guy with candy bar purchases. Sucking, coughing, and crying. *Man, we were so cool.*

Absently, I reach for the soft pack of Marlboro Lights before remembering, I don't like Marlboro Lights. I crumple the carton I my fist, a satisfying sense of gratification as I feel the four or five remaining stokes succumb to my grip. I toss it to the passenger side floor. I am oh-for-two this morning as far as vices go. No Coke, no Salem Menthols.

Pretty much indicative of this damn day.

12:03 p.m.

Up ahead on the left is the junior high where kids are playing on the soccer field in matching green t-shirts and black shorts, names emblazoned across their backs. "Smith", "Jones", and "Washington", become "Stevens", "Harris", and "Stoneham", as I recognize my friends in eighth grade gym class.

I see a nervous Freddy Stevens collecting soccer balls for Ms. Chambry, the TA we all had a crush on. As he approaches her, face flushed, arms stretched awkwardly around a full load of regulation sized balls, Rick Harris sneaks up behind him and pulls his shorts down with a two-handed tug. Balls roll everywhere as Freddy grabs to pull up his pants, underwear and all. Even in my black and white memory, his face is as bright red as the goalie pinny. *Good times.*

I didn't live close to this neighborhood, but it was on the way to friends' houses and downtown. I used to roam these blocks daily as a kid. Up and down the streets on my dirt bike, jumping curbs and spinning out on the blacktop. My legs ache to pump, to run, to pedal like a kid again. Instead, I adjust the a/c and drive on.

The street corners are the same, but different. Push button light switches adorn the poles. Heaven forbid you be expected to learn how to cross a street safely without instruction. The city has also installed planters along the sidewalks. More maintenance to cost more money that I'm sure the city doesn't have. State grants for planters while the school recycles their worn, graffitied desks for one more year.

I shake my head at my cynicism. *Shame on me.* Once they're filled and in bloom, the planters will be beautiful. Maybe just what some sad streetwalker needs to—I bark out a laugh. I crack myself up. I didn't mean prostitute, I meant lonely student ambling down the street or harried new mother pushing a stroller. Not that I would deny a hooker the pleasure of street bouquets.

Still smiling, I meander through the residential area, the atmosphere shifting subtly block by block. I pass Missy Butler's house and wonder if her family still lives there. Probably not since the lawn is mowed and there are no cars on jack stands in the cracked driveway.

I cruise by old man Carter's trailer, I'm sure he's still there. He fought tooth and nail for the right to live in a mobile home in the middle of houses. Was his property, he paid the same taxes, so why'd the damn city care? We kids were glad he won his fight. He gave out full-sized candy bars at Halloween. In hindsight, there's not much correlation there, but I guess if he'd lost, he would have moved and wouldn't have been around to award me with a full-sized Snickers on my favorite holiday.

I do love Halloween. Always have. I enjoy the ability to be someone, or something, else for a day and not have anyone question the who or why of it. One day a year, the mask comes standard.

This one year, I think it was maybe 1984, the guys and I were thirteen or fourteen, and we went as members of the fictional rock band, Spinal Tap. We couldn't tell our parents who we were dressing up as because the movie, *This is Spinal Tap*, was rated R and we were supposed to be watching *The Ice Pirates* when we sneaked into the next theater. As I recall, we all showed up at Rick's house dressed as pirates and adapted the costumes there. Now that I think about it, I'm positive that's what we did. Rick's parents never paid much attention to us.

At first, we considered all being a deceased Spinal tap drummer, there were like twelve of them and as many different ways to have died. But in the end, only Freddy went as a dead drummer. I think it was because Rick really wanted to stick a foil wrapped zucchini down his pants, but a bassist with three dead drummers seemed kind of dumb.

I shake my head, crank my tunes to *eleven*, and continue driving down memory lane. Next up, the historic district. Some of the houses here are really cool with cupulas and multi-colored paint jobs, but the neighborhood's claim to fame is my fellow classmate, Augie Sims, who shared a cell with famous defrocked televangelist Homer Grange. Remember him? He of the blood-crying wife? Red mascara, ha, wasn't even that great of a trick.

I vividly recall the late night church TV closing, "Get your Christ on before you sign-off." There would be a hymn and then the crucifix would fade into the no-signal snow. Pretty cool effects for back in the day.

I think that maybe if my classmate's parents had paid more attention to young Augustus instead of replicating the porch rail, spindle by authentically hand-shaped spindle, he wouldn't have felt the need to put a pipe bomb in the admin building. It's not like he knew attempting to blow up his father's work place would get him air time in the background of the Barbara Walter's interview with Homer Grange, so I have to believe there was supplementary motivation. If he's out in time, I'm sure he'll be Mr. Popularity as the class reunion, six degrees of television exposure and all that.

After passing by a few more blocks and revisiting a few more memories, I make my way to the stateliest of the local neighborhoods. Rick's neighborhood.

12:12 p.m.

Rick's street, no, boulevard, pronounce it *boo-leh-vahd*, is not like any place I ever lived. I know that there are kids in some of these houses, but not kids like I was a kid. I guarantee no one has ever played kick-the-can down this street or a game of pick-up soccer using the lily garden as goal. Of course, why would you play in the *boo-leh-vahd* when you could play on the estate? Half these houses probably have their own soccer fields or tennis courts. Not *or*, I correct, *and*. Soccer fields *and* tennis courts.

What I find ironic is that given the opportunity, heck, even the idea, of playing in the street, I think Rick would have jumped at the chance. I'm sure it would have been considered a bizarre form of rebellion. *Playing? In the streets?* How boorish. His parents and neighbors may have been shocked and embarrassed by such crass behavior, but it might have been good for Rick to act out in such a harmless manner. A poor man's revolt. Can't believe I'm just thinking of this now.

By the time I turn into Rick's driveway, I'm hyped on nostalgic overload. My senses are tingly with what had-been clashing with what currently-is, and perhaps even slammed by the idea of what's to-come.

Or it could be a toxic combo of no sleep, the mind-numbing dots of an 8 a.m. Scantron, an empty stomach, and shitty cigarettes.

12:15 p.m.

I haven't been here in years. Literally, years, but when I pull up to the parted gate and see the estate looming ahead, I feel sixteen again. Heck, if someone else was driving, I might feel like a wide-eyed twelve year old.

The reflections of the sun beating off the copper edging of the roof, the scent of a freshly mown lawn, although not Rick's I notice, and the shadows cast by the majestic abode, make my head spin in a veritable time-warp. The shag of his long grass and errant weeds impede the sound of my tires crunching over the imported lava gravel and I have an *a-ha* moment as I wonder why we never thought of driving on the grass during our wild days of sneaking in and out.

I inhale deeply and hold it for the time it takes to pull alongside the couple of other cars parked outside the multiplex they call a garage. I release my breath with a whistle, wondering how things can change, and not change, all at the same time.

The apron of marble stairs that lead to the double-wide arched front doors welcomes me back, with familiarity and in time. As I cross the driveway, I, too, cross back through history.

I met Rick the first day of seventh grade, another new town, another new school, another new friend. Back then, I just thought he was nice, reaching out to the new kid. I'd had

21

a lot of that over the years. You know, everybody wants to be first to feel out the new student; make sure he knows his place in the hierarchy. I assumed this "friendship" was no different.

Later, I would learn that I was more than just a novelty to him. Rick is a seeker of fresh and different experiences and my poor troubled ass was certainly fresh and different to him. Oddly enough, in me, he found the stability he secretly desired.

Back then, my mom was trying really hard to make a normal life for us. She'd joined the PTA, bought a bicycle so she could save gas and get exercise, and was working nights waitressing at the go-to spot for special occasions and celebrations, which left her afternoons free to drive me to classmates' houses.

A little intimidated by my choice of new friend, she'd considered parking on the boulevard, afraid of detracting from the million dollar domicile with her aged rattletrap. That would have meant nearly a quarter mile hike up the winding drive. In the end, she told me, "It's better to hide on the estate than advertise on the street."

It had been autumn then, but it still smelled like fresh cut grass. The sun reflecting off the roof edging had temporarily blinded me. I'd never seen anything like it and despite the discomfort, I couldn't look away. Such splendor, such magnificence. It was fancier that anything I'd ever seen, and at the time, I thought I'd seen a lot.

The same blinding flashes from the copper trim bloom in my view now. I approach the marble steps that lead to the entrance, impressed at how opulence never goes out of style.

How many photo ops did we have on these stairs? Every homecoming, prom, Sadie Hawkins dance and graduation. The girls in frilly dresses and fancy underwear. The guys in suits or tuxes, wallets fat with cash and condoms.

We all had that matching bulge in our back pocket, invisible accessories pilfered from older brothers, bathroom quarter machines, or those cocky enough to ask the school nurse. Regardless of the probability of the rubber being used, we were packin'. High school is a very optimistic time of sexual development.

And sexual tensions. The one and only time I was in a fistfight was also on these steps. Mickey Bland didn't like my snarky comment about his girlfriend, Sarah, "pulling a train". In my defense, I didn't know what it meant. Pardon my pun, but when I said it, I was totally on a different track.

We'd gone to the drive-in movie the week before and Sarah had been the lead car. She'd crawled up every frickin' aisle, row after row, before finally pulling into a space. About two feet from the playground! There were at least seven cars in our "train". See? And we'd ended up all parking where not only could we not see the screen, but the little kids screaming and laughing drowned out the speakers, too.

That evening on the stoop, I repeated the phrase I'd been told. By Rick. Rick who laughed his ass off as Mickey and I flailed like a couple of spazzoids. Swinging, slapping, and ducking. One punch. That's all Mickey connected. That's all it took. I went down like a drunk girl on prom night.

My tongue involuntarily touches the crag of the tooth I chipped when my face hit the marble, the back of my upper

23

lateral incisor. For anyone whose mother did not date a dentist, those are the teeth on the outside of your front teeth.

Gees, the dentist. We're just full of jolly memories today.

Standing in the shade thrown from an elaborate decorative cornice, happy to be out of the blazing sun and dazzling roofline, I take a moment to regroup. The past is not a good place for me to dwell. Not even the recent past.

12:20 p.m.

Bounding up the ten or so low stairs to the massive front doors, I pause again, wondering if I'm up for this. It's been a long time. I consider the potential distance that might have developed since I've been gone. Mental, physical, social growth. We've been apart almost as long as we were inseparable.

That's what people do, though, right? They grow up. Move on. I'm not sure what's weirder to me…that they never left or that I'm back.

But then I think, *what the hell?* What's the worst that could happen?

Thumbing the brass lever, I let myself into the residence as if I belong, my auto-pilot kicking in again. Familiarity, it seems, never forgets. It's weird being here after so much time has passed. Mostly because it doesn't seem weird at all. I spent half a dozen of my most formative years in this house.

The curved staircase steps are smaller than I remember, the smooth banister seemingly too narrow for a proper slide at my age and size. I notice there are several paintings missing from the wall, the wallpaper a little more vibrant in the recently revealed rectangles.

Walking down the upstairs hall, past alternating portraits and closed doors, I head to the room at the end. I rap on the slightly open bedroom door as I enter.

Hey theres and high-fives greet me.

Rick, Stoney, Freddy, and me. The Psychedelic Fours, back together again.

12:21 p.m.

"You're late," Rick says.

"Yes, late," Stoney repeats.

"He who comes too late is punished by life," Freddy offers in a Russian accent.

We all stare at him.

Rick clears his throat and begins again, "You're late—"

It takes me a minute before I realize why they're calling me out. I'm not *that* late. Then, the smile sliding across my lips suddenly becomes a grimace. I run my hands through my hair, grabbing fistfuls and tugging. I say, "You are not going to believe what happened…"

All three sit a little straighter, eyes focused on me, ready for the excuse I am about to provide.

I feign breathlessness, lending an air of urgency to my saga, which is easy to do because after a few inhales and exhales, I really am breathless. *Gotta cut back on the smokes,* I think.

I launch into a tale of demon-possessed university professors who turn their students into zombies for sport and tenure. After four dangerous years navigating the tenuous line between open-mindedness and controlled thought, I'd narrowly escaped a very progressive and evil instructor intent on my mental corruption. Or had I?

"Must…not…compromise…" I gasp. Jerking at the waist, arms extended, I roll my eyes back in my head. "Must terminate independence. Must convert brains to useless mush," I mumble, stepping further into the room. I rock awkwardly in a circle. "No mush-worthy brains to be found," I growl.

Stoney and Freddy applaud and I bow in appreciation of their praise.

"Zombies, huh," Rick says. "S'been done." But he claps anyway.

It's an old game we played when we were kids. Whenever one of us was late or in trouble, we'd make up some outlandish lie to cover our butts. For a while, Sophomore year, I think, Freddy was late on purpose just for the opportunity to be the center of attention and try out some new voices.

Me, I tried really hard to not be late or in trouble, my truths oftentimes more gruesome than our fabrications.

Conquering my gasps, I sit on the edge of a futon, forearms on my thighs, and lean into the group. "So, what'd I miss?"

"Nothing," mumbles Stoney.

"Nada," says a squeaky voiced Freddy.

"Nuttin' honey," Rick says, grinning. He flips a cigarette out of a pack and my hand is extended in request by the sight of the green and white box before the verbal appeal is even formed. So much for cuttin' back.

"Bum a smoke, man?" I ask even as he's tossing me the cellophane wrapped lung candy. Rick leans forward to light me with his trusty Zippo, an antique that belonged to his grandfather.

"Thanks," I say tightly before releasing my smoke-filled exhale. *That's the stuff.*

It's the first time the four of us have hung out together since, gees, I don't even remember. I think they've seen each other in different combinations during holiday breaks, long weekends, and summers, but I rarely partook. Having the "whole gang" together is kind of a novelty. And I mean novelty as in odd, not special. People change, history doesn't.

The room is palpable with conflicting pressures. Or maybe that's the smoke in my lungs. No, I definitely sense and urgency to renew our friendship, to pick up where we left off. An air of desperation, of *what now?*

I'm basically starting over. Again. New college down state in the fall for Grad school, new apartment, new responsibilities, new friends. It's something I've never gotten used to. Maybe I'm the source of angst? The pressure to revert to a safe zone emanates from me?

Their gazes all draw to my direction and I feel stifled. My mood does not mix well with the warm temps and high humidity. For as lavish as Rick's parents' house is, they've skimped on the air conditioning. More likely, they hadn't anticipated this unseasonably warm weather, from his vacation home in Sedona, or hers in the Virgin Islands, and haven't turned it on yet. Just one more pebble in the shoe of irritation that is this day.

"So, what's up?" I ask as I look for somewhere to flick my ash. I tap it on my pant leg, rubbing the offending light spot into blue jean oblivion. A memory floats to the forefront and holding up my smudged thumb, I ask, "Cheeky-cheeky anyone?"

There is a collective groan as I recall one of the first "real" parties I'd ever been to. It featured a very toasted Rick, a bunch of his friends from the club, and a memorable party game.

Rick had an entirely separate social circle through the country club. All of those kids went to the private academy, but since Rick's grandfather was an original sponsor of the "new" high school back in the early 60's, it became forever a Harris legacy to avail of a public education.

Stoney and Rick and I showed up at this guy's mansion, hoisting a sixer of Mickey's Big Mouth, and it was nothing like the Richie parties you see in the movies. The place was not packed with writhing, partially clad bodies. The music was not pulsating through the chandeliers. No hot adolescents were visibly humping. Instead, a handful of pretty people sat sedately in several rooms, sipping and chatting and laughing as U2 was piped through the surround sound at a moderate volume.

We walked into this dude's house, and Rick was all like, "hey, how you doin'?", and me and Stoney were just hanging back, ready for a quick retreat should anybody question our being there. We didn't know those people, but we knew Rick, and we'd seen him run people from his own house parties before.

But the guests who greeted us seemed pretty chill. They showed us the coolers—one with ice and cans of beer, the other filled with a very red fruit punch. Very red, like the color of your tongue after you eat a raspberry Razzle. The scent was strong and fruity.

We each dipped a cup and took a sip. It tasted like they mixed up a super batch of strawberry Kool-Aid and doubled the sugar to cover the taste of booze. It worked. I couldn't taste it, but it was in there. Later, my puke would stain the snow at the curb like a grisly murder scene.

The host, a guy named Andre that everybody called Frenchie, rounded up the guests, I'd say there were about twelve to fifteen of us. He had us sit in a circle on the living room floor. There was a comfortable buzz going, everyone seemed pretty mellow. Happy, content. Me and Stoney were feeling good—fitting in okay, not embarrassing Rick in front of his better friends.

"We're going to play a game," Frenchie announced. The crowd moaned and a couple people waved him off. "No, really, it'll be fun," he said, sitting down to complete the ring. "Everybody have a fresh drink? You don't need it for the game, but no interruptions once we start playing, okay?"

Nods all around.

"This game is called cheeky-cheeky." He scanned the circle. "Anybody played before?" A couple of people bobbed their heads, broad smiles on their faces. "Good, you guys can help make sure nobody cheats." He winked at a particularly comely girl seated to the right of Rick. "This game is super simple. I'm going to turn to the person to the left of me and say something like, cheeky-cheeky. Then, I'm going to pinch their cheek."

He turned to the guy beside him, said, "cheeky-cheeky", then pinched his cheek. The guy ducked out of his grip, the right side of his face brighter than the other. "Then he'll do the same to the person next to him, and so on and so on, until we get back to me. Then I'll change it up a bit. Super easy. Everybody ready?"

There were affirmations and guffaws.

31

"Cheeky-cheeky," he said, again grabbing and releasing that poor dude's cheek. That guy pinched the redheaded girl on his left, she tweaked the cheek of the blonde next to her who then nipped the cheek of the guy beside her.

"Cheeky-cheeky," she said, pinching his cheek and leaving a dark smudge. Everybody burst out laughing but the guy just turned to the next person and so on until the hot chick beside Rick pinched his cheek, also leaving a dark smudge. Again they laughed, but not me and Stoney. Oh, hell no, he was our ride home.

Rick laughed though and turned to pinch Stoney who pinched me and we kept it up until the circle returned to Frenchie.

"See?" Frenchie asked. "Easy as pie. Okay, let's try," he pondered, "eary-eary", and he tugged on the ear of the guy next to him. Again, the circle continued, partiers giggling over the silliness of saying "eary-eary", then laughing harder as the two people got smudged.

We repeated the game several times, "foreheady-foreheady", "eyebrow-eyebrowy", and finally, "nosey-nosey", where the first victim noticed the mark and swiped his face.

"What the hell," he shouted, standing and staring at his dirty fingers. He showed the crowd his soiled fingertips, like we weren't aware.

Everybody was laughing, Rick loudest of all. Before he could open his mouth to say something stupid, the other guy pointed at him and yelled across the circle, "What? What were you going to say? Get a mirror, buddy, that's what I say." Then he stomped through the living room into the kitchen and began scrubbing his face with a wet paper towel.

"What?" Rick asked, pulling himself to standing. His eyes were crossed as he tried to look at his own face. Finally, he took both hands and scrubbed them up and down his cheeks. They came away dirty. "What the fuck, Frenchie?"

People were openly enjoying this scene. Oh man, Rick hated that. Frenchie, still seated, told him to calm down. He raised and lowered his hand in a slowing motion.

"C'mon, Rick," he chortled, "it's all in good fun. And besides, it wasn't me." He pulled a wide-eyed innocent look and motioned toward the hot blonde still on the floor beside Rick's vacated spot. "Sherry is the one that cheeky-cheekied you. If you have a problem with the game, take it up with her."

Sherry adjusted her sitting position, tossed her hair, and threw her shoulders back, exposing more cleavage. "I'm sorry," she pouted. Rubbing her smudged fingertips together, she said, "It would take more than a smear of cigarette ash to make you unattractive."

And that was all it took. Suddenly Rick was smooth and suave and sliding back into the spot beside her. Fingering her hair and rubbing his cheek on hers. Mr. Fun Guy, life of the party, a great sport. He left the ash on his face for the rest of the night, commenting whenever he could about how clever that game was, how having two dupes was brilliant.

Stoney and I got the real Rick all the way home. He made us pull into an all-night Denny's to use their rest room and wash that shit off his face. I wish I'd have made it to the Denny's rest room. We never went to another of those parties again.

"Fucking ashtray scum! Those assholes! You assholes!" Rick cries in recollection.

"Yo, dude, what did you want us to do?" Stoney asks.

"Uh, tell me."

"Right. Tell you. In front of everyone. At a party where you were the only person we knew." I shake my head.

"You didn't seem to mind when you thought it was only on the other guy's face," Stoney says.

"Yeah," I say, "you seemed to think that was pretty funny."

"Fuck you. It was funny. On him."

"Remember a few months later when you tried to pull that same cheeky-cheeky shit at one of your parties?" We're all nodding. Of course he had Freddy sit next to him.

"Unfortunately for you and your party game," Freddy says as Oscar the Grouch, "I have a very keen sense of smell. I could tell right away that you had shit on your fingers."

"Ash," Rick says.

Freddy/Oscar laughs. "Right, because cigarette ash is way less gross than shit."

"It is," Rick says.

Stoney and I exchange a look and a grimace, imaging that version of the party game. *Assholey-assholey?*

Truth is, me and Stoney couldn't wait to share the ash story with Freddy. What voice did he do? I hear bells bong and think, *The more you know*, in the voiceover of the NBC promo ad.

12:35 p.m.

Individually navigating memory lanes, we sit in solitude again.

As far as I know, Rick was the first home from college and having had to wait the longest is definitely the most excited about this reunion. I think he's flunked out of another school, but I'm not sure. He doesn't bring it up and I don't ask.

I hear Stoney is on the extended education plan. I'm pretty sure he goes to the resident state school and still lives at home with his parents and sister. He takes a few classes at a time. His mom works in the career services office, so he gets cheap tuition. He was always a good student in high school, but because it came naturally, not because it was priority. I think he's still committed to his part-time job at Cleaver's Family Market. Back in the day, he had a thing for Andrea Cleaver, but it's been years. I'm not sure why he still works there, but I admire his dedication. I've never done anything that long.

"Famous" Freddy takes classes at the community college. Eight semesters in and I don't know if he's declared a major yet. He's the king of "almost". *No*, I think, not even. Maybe the prince, but probably the jester. Yeah, that sounds about right, the Jester of Almost. He *almost* passed that class.

He *almost* got that job. He *almost* lost his virginity. He doesn't expect to succeed, so he doesn't.

Except for the voices. We call him "Famous" because of the awesome impersonations he's always doing. We've told him since eighth grade that he should hone his comedic skills, make it work for him. But he doesn't have the confidence and we are too lazy, too distracted, and too selfish to do it for him.

The lull continues and I wonder why Rick pressed for this get together. "You know, the guys hanging out, just like old times." Be here by noon, he said. I guess we thought he had something planned. I guess we were wrong.

12:40 p.m.

Pleasantries exchanged, small talk exhausted, the four of us lounge around Rick's room waiting for someone to take charge.

"Going to graduation?" Stoney asks me, interrupting the silence.

"Naw."

"Hey there, pilgrim, how exactly am I supposed to live vicariously through you," John Wayne asks, "if you don't go on and graduate?"

"Oh, I'm graduating," I say. "I'm just not walking. You know they charge you for that shit? Er, I mean, *honor*."

"What's up with grad school?" Stoney asks.

"S-I-U," I shout rhythmically.

All three faces crinkle in response. "S-I-*ew*," Freddy says.

I shrug in response. "Gotta goes where theys pays me to goes."

"Pay you to go?" Suddenly Rick is interested.

"Well, not really," I begin, "but sort of, I guess. I have a full scholarship and depending on my professor recommendations, I'm pretty sure I'll have a TA position. That pays."

"Huh," Rick says, retreating back to his game of catch and release with what I am guessing is a dirty sock ball.

"That's cool, man," Stoney says.

And again we fall into that not-quite-but-almost-uncomfortable quiet. An abyss of opportunity lacking impetus.

I look around and take in the—what? Ambience hardly seems like the right word. The setting? Too broad. The atmosphere? Naw, simpler. I take in the room. The people. That's it. Naturalistic observation it's called, simply witnessing subjects in their natural environment.

Rick is sprawled across the king-sized bed. He's just shy of six feet tall, softer now than he was in high school. Lazy, not fat. The poster child for why P.E. should be required for life. I can't tell if his blonde mop needs a haircut or a shower, but he's looking rather Shaggy-ish today. Despite his classically handsome good looks—chiseled cheekbones, deep blue eyes, and strong jawline, respectable breeding stock—his drug use and all around languid lifestyle make him look older than he is.

Freddy is sitting cross-legged on the floor. He's still slight and scrappy. Dark hair, dark eyes, and pale skin, he hasn't changed at all since high school. Shit, he hasn't changed since eighth grade. *Poor guy.*

Stoney is propped up against the window frame. I catch him sneaking glances at Rick's younger sister, Michelle, who is sunning by the pool. Stoney still looks the same to me, too, but genetics were kinder to him than Freddy. He is tall and lanky, easily six foot four in his window slouch, with a new short haircut that makes him look like a grown-up. Professional.

I'm draped over the folded futon, stretched out in an attempt to keep cool. I'm not as tall as Stoney, but too tall for

38

this piece of furniture. A perpetual student, you'd be hard-pressed to find anything professional about me.

Considering how much my mom and I moved, it's kind of cool that Rick still lives in the same house where he grew up. *Right, like he's grown up.* I crack a secret smile. Still, must be nice to have a real home, the same room, a place to come between semesters and expulsions.

I heard his mom moved out and his parents are divorcing. Another of those subjects of which he won't bring up and I won't ask about.

Rick likes to think he's independent of his parents; their troubles, their rules, their expectations and opinions. But not their money. He's just a big spoiled kid. His parents were the type that substituted affection with stuff. Growing up, I was so jealous. I actually thought it was awesome that his 'rents ignored him, let him do pretty much whatever he wanted, and never had a problem financing his shenanigans.

I scan the room and sigh. We should have plenty to do with all of the big-boy toys available to us. There are multiple gaming systems, a television, a VCR, a CD player, a high-end stereo with gigantic subwoofers that would not have fit in my room even if they were the only things in there, and a seemingly endless supply of porno mags.

Seriously, the magazines are everywhere. I shoved five or six off the futon before I sat down. Just thinking about it makes me feel dirty. I am suddenly stricken with a strong desire to stand, wipe off and then scrub my hands with disinfectant.

My point is that we are young, free for the moment from responsibilities, and immersed in a testosterone playground, yet we are cumulatively bored. And Rick is playing with a dirty sock ball. Suddenly, the skin mags make the sock ball even more disgusting. I want to scrub Rick's hands with disinfectant, too.

As we lay sulking, playing a round-robin of, "I don't know, what do *you* want to do?" I try to encourage spontaneity by reminiscing.

12:44 p.m.

"Still got my halo," I say, pulling one last drag on my second Salem.

As I'm disposing of the filter in an empty Mountain Dew bottle, I see Stoney shaking his head, a smirk touching the corner of his lips.

"Ex-squeeze me? Baking powder?" says Freddy in the stoner voice of Wayne Campbell.

"No way!" says Rick in a decent mimicry of the Mike Myers character.

"Way!" I say in my best Garth, which isn't very good.

We all laugh as Freddy wiggles his hands up and down and makes doodly doodly doo sounds indicating a dream sequence. "Hey Wayne, Garth," he says, "I loved my 'O' so much…"

He pauses, waiting for one of us to pick up the next line. Stoney, in his own voice, complies. "Why didn't you marry it, then?"

I remember that Freddy left his "O" on the back porch so his dad wouldn't see it and someone stole it.

"Wish I had," Freddy says as a sad Wayne.

"Ah, stop," Rick cuts in. "You'd have pawned it by now anyway, Fred."

"Not pawned," I say. "Held it for ransom!"

Stoney laughs at that. "How much you think they'd have paid for its safe return?"

Rick snorts. "Cheaper to replace it. Pretty sure by then, they'd started buying in bulk."

The "O" I have is the first of the giant letterforms. About twenty-two inches high, mine is solid steel painted with a gold epoxy, and weighs in at a good twenty pounds. The four of us stole it from the Split Mound Country Club. We thought we were so clever.

Originally, it was Rick's idea. He cared less about what happened to the letter than the fact that it called out its members as cunts. Even though he was one of them, the only reason any of us were allowed on the property. I caddied there one summer, worst summer of my life. Well, not worst summer so much as worst job. They really are cunts.

Rick's dad was all concerned because the "O" had slipped down a few inches from the rest of the letters. He went on and on about shoddy workmanship and club credibility and blah, blah, blah. So, Rick decided to shut his dad up. He golfed late one night while I caddied for him. In an escapade worthy of *Ocean's Eleven*, I fancy myself Dino, we pried it off with a 9-iron, hid it under a blanket on the cart, then tossed it over the fence to where Stoney and Freddy were waiting. They caught it in a tarp, wrapped it up and stuck it in the trunk of Stoney's Volkswagen Beetle. I got the first one because Rick couldn't exactly bring it home.

"You take that "O"?" Freddy asks in a gruff voice eerily akin to Rick's father, Mr. Harris.

"Who, me?" replies Rick, placing his hands together before encircling his head with one and then returning them to a prayer position, batting thick lashes around wide eyes. Not getting caught was part of the halo legacy.

After a photo of the "new", we'd say "improved", signage was featured in the local paper, an outraged club board had it replaced within days. We considered that a fresh challenge and stealing the "O" kind of got to be our thing.

Stoney acquired the second one, but his dad found it and freaked out. "Hey, Stone, remember when your old man demanded you return your halo?"

We all nod as we traverse a shared memory.

"Yeah," Stoney grins. "That was like a scene from *Ocean's Eleven*."

I bark out a laugh. "I was just thinking that!"

"Dibs on Dino," Rick says.

Right, I think, but I don't respond.

"Man," Stoney says, shaking his head, "it was harder getting it back on to club property than it was getting it off."

Freddy also remembers. "Jou guys," he says in the accented voice of Pepe LePew, "vous puez, pee-ew."

"Come on, Fred," Stoney says jovially. "You were the superstar that day! I literally could not have done it without you."

It's true, Freddy was the star. He was buried up to his armpits in the dumpster, but still, the star.

My part was to tell Angie, one of the summer staff cooks, that my friend Rick, you know, *Rick Harris*, of course she knew Rick Harris, oh my god, wow, *the* Rick Harris, liked her and wanted to meet her after work by the third hole. I told her I'd cover her clean-up but she better go, go quickly.

So, while Rick was at the third hole playing kissy-face with Angie, and I was in the kitchen washing dishes, Stoney backed his car up the employee entrance drive, mostly for a fast getaway since the trunk was in the front of the car.

Freddy and Stoney were unloading the "O" when all of a sudden, Henry, my boss, a true cunt, came yapping through the kitchen door looking for Angie. Stoney peeled out of there, and in a panic, Freddy and I tossed the letter into the dumpster. With no place to hide, Freddy followed it in.

"And, I'm pretty sure," I add, "the one who stunk was pee-*you*."

We all laugh at this, even poor Freddy.

After Henry left, an excruciating twenty minutes later, I helped Freddy out of the trash pit, damp and smelly. We left the sign in the garbage can. Stoney's dad didn't say how we had to return it, just that we did.

The club found it and returned it to its place on the ivy covered brick wall. We tried to steal it again but they'd secured it too well and we ruined it trying to pry it off. Gouged it practically into a "Q". We considered taking another letter, but what's funny about Split Mund?

The next replacement "O" was fiberglass. Looked good up, matched well, but was cheap and flimsy. Popped off as easy as candy buttons. That's the one that was stolen off Freddy's porch.

A silence follows our storytelling. I feel like I'm further removed from these stories because these guys never left, but maybe not. Time is time.

"Hey," Rick says, "remember that day we had my dad's driver, Max, take us to Six Flags? Man, that was so much fun."

"Yeah," I say, "until Max got called into the city for a client and left us stranded."

"Aw, c'mon, that was part of the adventure!" He chuckles in that perfectly entitled way only country clubbers and Thurston Howell can. "What were we, fourteen? Fifteen? Not old enough to drive."

"Fifteen," says Stoney. "That was the summer I started working at Cleaver's. Remember? Cause I didn't get to go."

"Well, ah, well ah, you sort of got to go, to come, to be there," says Freddy, not making eye contact, a la Dustin Hoffman as Rain Man. "Yeah, you got to come and get us, get us, yeah. Get us."

"Oh, that's right!" shouts Ricks, slapping his forehead and rolling over onto his back. "I forgot about that part."

"My dad was *not* happy about that. Tell me again why you couldn't just call *your* dad, Rick? Or Max? Or one of his other lackeys?"

Rick turns to me, "We could have called your dad-of-the-week."

"Don't be a dick."

"I don't think we could've called Dick Randolph, he wasn't around until prom time."

"Fuck you."

"Fuck you, too?" He seems to ponder. "No, I'm pretty sure that Mr. Fukuto, the science teacher, wasn't until junior y—"

"Seriously, Rick, what's your deal?" I snap.

"Rick Deal, hmmm, that one doesn't ring a bell," Rick says, rubbing his chin in contemplation. "But, Rick Bell, he was the dentist, right?"

"Shut up," Stoney cuts in. "Seriously, you got them into that situation, why couldn't you, or your dad, get them out?"

"And," I interject; verging on pissed, "what's with your obsessive inventory of my mother's boyfriends?"

Rick dismisses me with a shrug and turns to Stoney. "Shit, I don't know. That was years ago. You know how my dad was. Is."

Harrumphing under his breath, Stoney returns to gazing out the window.

This is as uptight as I've ever seen Stoney. I am curious as to what's up with the dad-bashing.

"Hey," Stoney says, "remember when your sister was little?"

"What's that supposed to mean?" Rick asks, sitting up, slipping on a porno, righting himself with a jerk.

"Nothing," he says, never taking his eyes off poolside. "I'm just saying she's not a little girl anymore is all."

I get up and walk over to the window. Michelle is winter-pasty in her neon bikini. I hope she's wearing sunblock or she'll be lobster-rosy soon. She's so skinny I can see her ribcage from here. The hollows of her neck seem deep enough to hold water. But not the pool water, I hope, since it's a flourishing algae color.

"Wow," I say. "What's up with Michelle?" Three years younger than us, the last time I saw her, she was tan and robust and blossoming. Never one to be intimidated by her brother, or his friends, she was wild and outgoing and whip smart.

"Hands *and* eyes off Michelle," Rick growls.

46

Stoney's stare swings around and lands squarely on Rick. "Didn't seem to be a problem for you when it was my sister," he says.

"Yeah, well, your sister came on to me. How is Samantha, anyway?" he asks, a leer in his voice. "Wham-bam, thank you Sam!" Rick looks around at us, seeking comedic accolades. He gets none. "Whatever. It was a long time ago and it didn't mean anything." He hops back into a sitting position against the headboard, his legs sprawled.

"Dude," I shout, holding a hand up to block the immediate view. "Put some underwear on."

Rick looks down at his crotch. "What, this?" he asks as he yanks his nylon gym shorts to the side letting his junk dangle freely.

I notice Stoney turn away, too, but Freddy adjusts for a better view.

"I crap bigger than you," he rumbles in the voice of Jack Palance.

"Shut up, freak," Rick says. "Famous? Shit, we shoulda called you Freaky Freddy." He slides off the bed and kicks at a pile of dirty laundry. Then he opens a drawer, closes it, opens another. "Fuck." He flings open the walk-in closet door and disappears for a minute, yanking baggy cargo shorts up over the other pair as he emerges.

My stomach growls, loudly. Freddy acts like he's experiencing an earthquake. Grinning, I ask, "Hey, Rick, think Lupita would mind whipping up something for lunch?"

A hush fills the room like quicksand. I don't know how to interpret it, or the looks on the faces of my friends, but I can feel it, heavy and sucking.

"What?" I ask.

Stoney clears his throat. "Lupita, ah, well—"

"Loopy has left the building," Freddy says as Ed Sullivan.

I move to the edge of the futon, gripping the seam of the skimpy padding. She hated that nickname. "No way!" I say. "Why? Wait, she didn't…die or anything, right?" I can't imagine the Harris household without Lupita. She was amazing. The maid, chef, caregiver, boo-boo kisser, bail money provider. Barely ten years older than us, she was the most responsible grown-up in the whole family.

Rick grunts in response and lies back down on the bed. "She's not dead. She just," he pauses, "she got a better offer, I guess."

"Better offer?" I'm flabbergasted. "Better than," I begin, but then I consider all of the shit that Rick and his sister, and probably the missus and mister, too, put that poor woman through.

Stoney clears his throat and says, "Stuff has happened since you've been gone. Things have changed."

12:55 p.m.

"So catch me up," I say, resuming my reclined seat on the futon. I want to know, I do. Mostly I want to know why I'm here. Why any of us are here. Not in an existential way. Why Lupita isn't. I'm starving.

Suddenly, from the bed, Rick starts jabbering. Seems he was cut from his fraternity. Again. For good this time. They're telling him his brotherhood won't transfer to the next college.

The next college, I think. Shit, Rick is like the Gerald Ford of higher education. Never actually elected, or in Rick's case, applied and accepted. If it wasn't for his financial legacy, he'd be flipping burgers for minimum wage. That's assuming he has the ability, and inclination, to learn how to flip burgers.

As I listen to him, an involuntary sigh escapes. His conative tendencies to justify his cognitive and affective functions are mind-blowing. Actions and repercussions, man. The rest of the world functions on this simple premise.

I guess there were some trumped-up drug charges this time. "What a joke," he says, not joking. Not because he wasn't caught passing out drugs to some teenage girls that crashed a party, 'cause he did that, but the kicker was that another guy in the house sold the drugs to him. And how was he supposed to know the girls were only fifteen? Who invites

49

baby-bait to a college party? "That guy should be kicked out, that's for sure. Kicked out, shit," he continues, mumbling, "banished. For life."

Kicked out? Banished? Oh no, not that! A time-out in the corner for him. How about a jail sentence? How about a real punishment?

Rick is agitated, really caught up in this story. He's sitting up and kicking magazines aside. I'm glad he put on pants. He leans against the massive headboard, crushing a pillow to his chest. Here comes the rant. This is typical Rick behavior. I steel myself for the wave of self-pity that is surely about to carry us downstream, to the dam of disappointment. I close my eyes and conjure a toddler kicking and crying on the grocery store floor because mommy said no to a candy bar. *Poor Rick.*

He goes off on the stupidity of fraternities, the hypocrisy and back-stabbing, etcetera, etcetera. I'd roll my eyes, but they are still closed.

"It's such bullshit," he whines. "Organizations, groups, clubs...anything governed...such complete and total bullshit."

"Every government degenerates when trusted to the rulers of the people alone," Freddy says stoically.

"Who was that?" I ask, not recognizing the voice or the accent.

"Who cares," says Rick.

"Thomas Jefferson," Freddy answers, sitting a little straighter and introducing himself matter-of-factly.

"Fuck," I say with a chortle. "How would you possibly know what Thomas Jefferson sounds like?"

Freddy shrugs and we all kind of laugh.

The room is quiet for a moment as surely we all reflect on the vocal patterns of long dead president.

"Anyway," Rick says, diverting attention back to himself. "I can't believe they'd dare ban me. Me! I am a legacy to that house. My father was in it and his father before him. Gees, that house should be named after us."

"Kappa Upsilon Nu Tau?" Stoney offers.

I snigger, envisioning the letters KUNT over the ornate wooden doors of the beer stained cesspool that is every frat house I've ever been in.

"Seriously," Rick says, tossing a pillow in Stoney's direction. "We've dumped so much money into that glorified organization, it should be called..." He pauses, struggling with the Greek alphabet. "Arrr...Rho! Rho...H...Ha..." He stops speaking and shakes his head. "Whatever the fuck Richard Harris would be in Greek."

The idea of 'we' having 'dumped so much money' is not lost on his listeners, but really, it's Rick, Richard Harris the Third to be specific, so what's the point? He believes what he wants to believe. His perceptual issues are the result of arrested sensory modalities. Truth by association. You see that a lot in certain personality types, especially those whose implicit attitudes are allowed to cultivate unchecked.

That's textbook bullshit, I think. We all suffer from truth by association. It basically boils down to 'you learn what you live'. Yes, I earned a Bachelor of Science in Psychology, but I could've just as easily read it on a fortune from a cookie.

I ponder Rick's attributes for a long moment. He's really not *all* bad. I mean, he is who he is, but he's done good stuff, too. He took me in. And Stoney. And even Freddy. Sure, he can be mean, but he's also kind of...I dunno...needy. We each seem to bring our own deficits to the party, share the debits, spread the emotional debt. A vast wealth of fucked-upedness.

But, when it comes to Rick's wealth, literally, like dollars and cents and picking up the check, financially, even though he might hold it over us, he never actually withheld.

Of course, he never withheld an opinion, either.

"I hate fucking organizations," Rick says loudly, in case we forgot he was the center of the universe. "Remember when we were in the Cub Scouts?" He scowls to his captives, a sour memory. This is before my time, but I, too, know the story. We shrug unanimously. *Yeah, we remember*, our body language reports. We remember and we know where this is heading.

"Alamo, asshole," I say.

"Fucking Cub Scouts," he continues, "it's like eighth grade, man, and they won't let us bring liquor to the hayrack ride?"

"Dude," Stoney cuts in, needing to set the record straight. Again. "It was fifth grade. We were *eleven*. It was a 'habitats hike'. We were supposed to be looking for animal homes in nature. Not getting wasted and throwing up in a woodchuck hole."

Oh no, I think, shaking my head. I look in the direction of the window where Stoney's form is outlined by high daylight and mentally shout, *Why Stoney, why?*

"Alamo," I repeat.

"Aw, that's right!" Rick squeals. "Woodchuck!" He laughs and shoves a pillow behind his back, propping himself up against the monster headboard. "I remember now, that was so funny! Upchucking in the woodchuck hole. How much chuck could a woodchuck chuck…" He loses it, cackling and hugging himself with glee.

I continue to shake my head and mouth, *Alamo*. That was our code for somebody who's telling a story you've already heard. You know, no one wants to repeat the Battle of Alamo, the attack during the Texas revolution where most every soldier lost their life. It was pretty fucked up the first time, truly not worth repeating. So, yeah, we learned more history from a Pee Wee Herman movie than we did in the classroom.

The effect of his hilarious recall has passed and Rick reaches over and grabs a remote from his night stand. He presses some buttons and the room fills with music. Prince. *Cream*. Rick is so immature. Still, we all bob our heads and mouth the words.

Freddy selects a magazine from the tableside, a lusty busty bodacious edition. I stare intently, eyebrows raised in anticipation. He holds it by the edges, not the spine, a risky move if you ask me, and fans himself vigorously.

I remember my fourth grade teacher telling us that you expel so much energy fanning yourself, regardless of the cooling sensation; you are actually making yourself warmer. I keep my lesson to myself, adjusting my head in the crook of my arm and closing my eyes again. Science be damned, I'm a little jealous of Freddy's breeze.

The frat thing is really bothering Rick. He brings it up again. Or maybe again is the wrong word since he never left it. "Those fuckers," he mutters, head twitching. "Can't believe they'd throw me out. To the curb, man." The twitches grow into full head swings, back and forth. Denial, we'd call it, righteous indignation he'd say. The cognitive distortion of minimization, Dr. Henry, my psych prof would have said.

"As if I wasn't having enough trouble with classes," he continues, and I think, *ah, yes, flunking class is secondary college strife for Rick,* "they go and fuck up my home life." He stares at his hands as they clench and relax. "I loved that house. More of a home than this dump." He punches a fist into the disheveled covers.

We remain quiet. I ponder his histrionic personality and maladaptive tendencies. Do I have a solution? Advice to offer? Do I need an advanced degree for that? No, this is merely a vent and release party. He's not looking for answers, just a sounding board. My job is to let it happen.

"What is it with organizations and their fucking rules? Why can't there be a club for *me*?" He looks around, like he just remembered he's not alone. "For people like me," he begins, then, "for me and my friends," he amends. "For us."

This guy would make a stellar psychological study.

A thought flies through my head and out my mouth so fast that I'm not sure where it came from. "Where're Lexi and Rollie?" I ask, rocking into a seated position.

They look at me, six eyes, three furrowed brows, two mouths agape, one clenched tightly.

"Fuck you," Rick says, unclenching long enough to spew the words at me.

"What?" I am genuinely perplexed. Rolex, "Rollie", and Lexus, "Lexie", are the Harris' two wolfhounds. Gorgeous dogs. Big, lanky, smart. Man, I loved those dogs like they were my own.

54

Stoney clears his throat and says, "Rollie died. Hit by a car or something." I notice the *or something* is kind of mumbled. "Lexie went—"

"My fucking mom took my fucking dog when she fucking moved out. There, you happy? Thanks for fucking reminding me." Rick flings himself back and the headboard thumps the wall.

I quickly wonder if that was the "better offer" that Lupita got, too. I know he misses the dog more than his mother and I'm truly sorry for having said anything. It's just weird, is all. I mean, those dogs were part of our life here. Can't believe it took me this long to notice their absence.

"Like I said, things have changed." Stoney sighs and seems to shrink against the window frame.

Holy shit, what's going on? Again, I recline as best I can, eyes closed. I consider potential excuses to get out of here, get on with my day, with my life. *I got shit, too, you know. Things have changed for me, too. You have no fucking idea.*

"You should start your own," Freddy says. He utters it exactly like the wheelchair guy who talks through the computer.

Rick is still pissed that I reminded him about the dogs. "What?" he snaps. "What the hell are you talking about?"

"You should start your own," Freddy repeats in that mechanical voice. "You should start your own club." It's disturbing. The notion and the voice. It gets my eyes open and I stare at him, stare at him hard.

Like an automaton, he says, "It is new. I have been work ing on it. What do you think?"

I tell him, "It's eerie, man, but you do it really well. What's that guy's name, anyway?" The one you sound like?"

"Step hen Hawk ing."

"Oh, yeah, that's right. Now cut it out." I'm still looking at him, creepily impressed.

"Okay, enough with the vocal retard." Rick has never had an appreciation for Freddy's talents, even though he's the one that dubbed him *Famous*. "What did you say?" he demands of Freddy. "And say it normal."

His face twisting as if he'd just sucked a lime, in a pitch perfect tribute to Rick, Freddy says, "Start...your...own, man."

Missing the delivery completely, Rick sits forward, tossing the last pillow to the floor. "Oh my god, yes! That's a great idea. I'd hug you...but then I'd have to kill you." Rick is practically giddy. He's bouncing on the bed with overzealous enthusiasm. "We should! Do it, you know. Start our own club. Like a secret club."

That is a great idea, I think caustically. *Because we are twelve years old and secret clubs are the key to happiness.*

1:06 p.m.

At first, it was just Rick nattering on about how cool it would be to start his own club.

Then Freddy caught his enthusiasm faster than an STD in a whorehouse and joined him on the king-sized bed for proper planning.

We'd have a secret word—like on Pee Wee's Playhouse, for greetings and hot dates. That conversation was a bloated digression, featuring a very animated Freddy, as you can imagine.

There'll be a secret code and a secret sign and secret handshake, all basically used to show those not in the secret club how exclusive the club is. And also, to let everyone know if one of us is going to get lucky.

Rick is throwing down signs so fast I expect him to poke his own eye out. Fingers flying as he tries to create the perfect secret shake. Because he is *gonna get lu-u-ucky*.

Freddy is on board right away. I mean it was his idea, but if Rick hadn't run with it, he would have let it go. No, that's not completely fair. Freddy doesn't actually know what a good idea is until someone else comes up with it, even if it was his own. Because that's how Freddy is, has always been. That *almost* thing, again.

Stoney is quiet, because that's how Stoney's always been. The contemplative one, meditative and thorough. He of the balanced mind.

I'm not participating because I'm still trying to figure the best way out of here. *Got to get home to mommy?* No one would believe that. *Got a date?* Unlikely. *Late for work?* Ha, even more farfetched. The truth is, I've got nothing better to do. Maybe I should consider this club thing, might be fun. But no, I mean, what'd be the point? We haven't seen each other in months, years even, so why would we, the four of us, form a club. I interrupt their tete-a-tete. "Hate to be a buzzkill, because you two are obviously buzzed, but why the fuck would we start a secret club?"

Stoney snorts in agreement.

Both the bed bouncers stop cold at my comment.

"Because," Rick says, his tone injured, "we can."

I can tell I am thisclose to being uninvited to participate.

"And we should," concurs Woody Allen, as Freddy pushes up invisible glasses.

I shrug, not an easy feat considering my posture on the pseudo couch. With a twirl of my hand, I say, "Carry on."

The conversation between Rick and Freddy continues as if there'd been no ludicrous interruption on my part. It seems to snowball further, escalating to a near state of mutual euphoria.

The more they discuss, the more excited they get, the more distracted I become. I'm pretty sure I miss entire chunks of conversation because I am so busy mocking them in my head. They probably think I am smiling at their brilliance. I'm not.

I wonder how I got to twenty-two with these guys still in my life. I wonder if they are still in my life. Does today count? Initial nostalgia aside, do I even still know them? Do they know me? Did they ever really know me?

Every once in a while, I hear Stoney's voice as he tries to interject some sense into the conversation, but they will have none of that. *Sense?* Hell no. *Maturity?* Not to be had. *Reality check?* Ain't nobody cashin' that.

Got to give them kudos for their depths of creative boredom.

Rick is gunning for some sort of initiation to make it a *real* secret club.

"No!" he shouts. "Not a *club*." He rejects the word like it's gone rancid on his tongue. "A gang!" He regroups on the center of the bed, comforted by his newly inspired genius. In a hushed voice, he says, "We'll start our own *gang*." Eyes wide, he nods to each of us. "Way cooler."

As Rick's head bobs, Stoney, Freddy and I all shake ours side to side.

"Are you nuts?" Stoney asks with controlled tone. "We can't start a gang. Gangs are bad. Turf wars and shit. Last year there were thirteen deaths in Aurora that were gang related." I swear he whispers *dumbass* under his breath.

"Been stocking the papers again, Stoney?" Ricks chides, then continues as if no one had tried to derail his brilliant plan. "For real, this is such an awesome idea."

Out of the corner of my eye, I see Freddy puff up a bit.

"We need an initiation, though. All gangs have 'em. You need to prove your allegiance, your street cred."

Street cred?

He keeps talking about how we'll take it more seriously if we have to earn admission. Sort of like initiation at the fraternity, only not, you know, because lighting candles, wearing hoods, and chanting, is stupid. We have to prove our commitment, even if it's only open to the four of us, and it would be, no one else is worthy. No hazing, though, because that shit is whack.

They're kicking around some ideas: spray paint the dam, steal the "O", rob the Dog 'n' Suds, and finally I interrupt and say I have a suggestion. The three of them look at me expectantly, expecting to reject it, I'm sure.

I sit up straight, adjusting my height to the depth of the futon, my butt sinking well below the bend of my knees, and I begin to tell them how I went to do laundry late last night. They know I've moved out of my apartment since I've graduated. It stands to reason that I wouldn't want to pack dirty clothes.

I tell them how when I got to the laundry room with my basket crammed with basically everything I own, at least five normal loads worth of dirty clothes, which would also be crammed into one washer, maybe both if they were available, weighing a crap-ton and I'll be damned if both machines aren't in use. I hate that. I purposely wait until after midnight to go down to the inconveniently located laundry room at my apartment complex so I can be guaranteed a machine. Then they're both taken and no one is even there to let me know how long I'm gonna have to wait. Goddamn selfish jag-offs.

"I was pissed as fuck. It'd already been a long day. I was so tired. Mentally and physically exhausted. Toast, you know? I had two tests and a project due, my mind was fried.

I had one final left, first thing in the morning, and then I was heading straight home," I say. "Here," I revise, "heading straight here.

"I hadn't brought my books or notes, they wouldn't fit in the damn basket," I tell them, "so I can't even study while I wait for these thoughtless assholes to finish their wash after midnight on my last day here. Where are they anyway? I mean, how rude to just leave your stuff. I don't leave my stuff! Sure, I have better things to do, who doesn't?" I pause to catch my breath. "Actually, I was looking forward to a catnap on the folding counter while my laundry cycled." I smile dreamily at the idea of passing out on the table with the fresh scent and rhythmic swish of laundry, then shake myself out of it. "Every time I do laundry," I continue, "I think how crazy inconsiderate of the complex to only have two washers for like forty units. Stupid cheap-ass facility. At this point, I am hating on everything." I can see my audience nodding with understanding. "I wasn't going to leave my clothes and I wasn't going to lug that two-ton crap basket all the way back to my apartment to drag back later. When? After one? Two? Shit, my exam was at eight!"

I try to calm myself, take another breath and continue. "About ten minutes into my growing fucked-up mood, the timer on one of the washers dings. Hot damn, thank god. I pulled the damp clothes out, shoved—wedged—mine into the machine, dumped the last of my soap, tapping the box for every last powdery remnant. Then I grabbed my wire hanger to rig the machine." I pause for effect which takes great effort as the words want to burst from my mouth. "Only to realize that I can't." I take a breath before launching into the next part of my story. "Fuckin' management must've figured

61

out the scam because they have fixed the slots so that I can't stick the end of my untwisted wire and wiggle it to score a free wash. Fuck." I shake my head vigorously, remembering my initial reaction. "One…last…load…and *now* they fix it? What the hell?"

I'm on a roll, I can't stop talking. "I never pay! I never anticipate paying. I don't have any friggin' quarters on me. I don't have any money at all. I'm a starving Psych major for Christ's sake. I have a hanger! FUCK. I'm really pissed. I swat my thigh with the length of useless wire which hurt like a sonofabitch and pushed my pissiness to levels even I am unfamiliar with. We're talking code red on the apocalyptic frustration meter." Subconsciously, I rub my thigh; we all feel the sting.

At this point in my story, Rick interrupts. I halfway expect him to say, *Alamo,* just to be a dick. "What does this have to do with the club? Seriously, what's this have to do with anything?" he asks. "Because if you are trying to say we should wash clothes as initiation, well, that's just really lame."

Stoney takes the words right out of my mouth, "Shut up, Rick."

I keep talking, exposing them to my atomic anger, using big words and collegial dialect and short little meaningful street lingo to try and explain *exactly* how irritated I was.

"Then," I tell them, "I heard a car door slam nearby and I saw this guy walk past the laundry room entrance. I stepped outside and asked him if I could borrow a dollar, four quarters if he's got 'em. This guy was shitfaced drunk. I could smell it. Strong, like flammable from here." I motion to the space between me and Stoney. "And he was having

62

trouble keeping his balance," I continue. "He started swearing at me, *How dare I ask for a buck?!* Like a dollar would break him, he is his fancy suit and shiny shoes that probably cost more than my fucking car. I'm wondering what he's doing slumming around a college apartment complex at this time of night in this condition and conclude he is up to no good. He was still yelling, stumbling closer. Calling me lazy, good for nothing, a son of a bitch Then he called me a—" I choke on the next word, "bastard." Swallowing hard, I continue, "He's waggling his bony finger at me." I mimic him, making my voice high and sluggish. "He knowsh kidsh like me," I slur.

Freddy is nodding empathetically, eyes wide, waiting for some comeuppance. I'll be the hero in my story like he's never been in his.

"This little guy called me a loser scamming by on hard working Americans like himself. Then he poked me with that same boney finger, reaching up to do it." I rub my chest. "Suffer from short man syndrome much? God." I shake my head and cluck my tongue. "When he jabbed that little finger in my chest, trying to emphasize how much better he was than me and called me a worthless son of a bitch, I just snapped." My finger goes from a poking motion to a snap. "Before I knew what I was doing, I had the wire hanger wrapped around his neck and I was pulling and squeezing with a crazy angry strength. Tighter and tighter. He struggled, all sloppy with drunk weight, damning himself. He shut up then, stupid fuck. Shut up and fell to the ground."

I stop talking. Take a breath. My whole body is agitated; I can feel my pulse pounding through my major organs, blood carried on spikes of adrenaline through my veins. Face

63

flushed, internal temps matching external enervation. My hands are shaking. I look around, taking in the expressions on their faces. Wide with shock, astonishment, and disbelief. I watch their eyes as they process what I've told them.

Rick scoffs. "Is this one of those 'you'll never believe what happened' stories?"

My spell is temporarily broken. In reprieve, I shrug.

"No, really," Freddy asks as the television pitchman. "Inquiring minds want to know."

"I don't think he's lying," Stoney says. His penetrating eyes stare me down.

I shrug again and take in a cleansing breath, trying to steady my limbs. I try on a smile and wave my hand at their questioning faces. "Yeah, yeah, yeah. Just a story." I adjust myself in the futon, crossing a long leg over one knee. "You'll never believe…" my voice trails off as my breathing calms.

I can see the shift in their eyes as they collectively go from disbelieving awe to hesitant acceptance to hmm…maybe…

Rick readies a cigarette for me, but I dismiss the offer. My hands are clutching the cuff of my jeans, I'm not sure I could hold a cigarette steady enough to light it.

It's Stoney who says, "Go on."

"What?" I affect a vacant visage. "You know, zombies and shit," I add with a forced chuckle.

"C'mon," Rick says, an eerie calm to his voice. "Tell us what happened."

So I tell them the rest. Unsteady at first, but once my fury resurfaces, it drives my story. I tell them how I dragged that asshole back to his car, frisked his pockets for the car keys, propped him in the passenger side, then shut the door. How I went back and collected my laundry from the machine, dry but coated in a grainy film of detergent, jammed it all back into my basket and walked as fast as I could to my apartment.

"I jogged back to the parked car, thankful for the first time that those jackass laundry squatters were still taking their sweet time. I drove him to the other side of town, pulling into an old overgrown lot a few blocks from a bar. I hoisted his scrawny butt over the console and swung his legs to the driver's side then reclined the seat. Just some drunk guy sleeping off a bender. Who happened to get violated by some young street punk looking for a quick score. What has this country come to when a guy can't sleep off a bender in a vacant lot?

"I wiped everything down as best I could. Does that even matter?" I ask them in all honesty. "I mean, I don't have a record." I look at Rick. "Despite your greatest teenaged efforts to incriminate me—" I look to Stoney, then Freddy, "us," I add and laugh uneasily. "Efforts to incriminate us. Anyway," I shake my head, "I've never been fingerprinted." I try to laugh again but a dry *chuh* us all that comes out. "What I mean is, they wouldn't know it was mine even if they found a print, right? But I've seen enough episodes of *Twenty-one Jump Street* to know to wipe. I pulled the hanger down my shirt, too, and I left it in the car. Let them believe it was a carjacking gone wrong or something. Yeah, like someone tried to steal this dude's car, it was a nice car, and then when they found him passed out inside, they tried to rob him and when he woke up, they killed him. It kind of makes sense," I say, talking myself through it, trying to convince someone, anyone, me.

"None of it makes sense!" I shout. "But it could happen, right?" My eyes are burning. They feel small, tight and dry. "Shit, I don't care what the cops think. Just don't let them think it was me."

My mouth is parched and my words are sticking to my tongue. I can't believe I'm telling them this. Rick opens the mini-fridge by his bed and tosses me a cold Mountain Dew. I roll the icy wet bottle over my forehead, using the droplets as an excuse to rub my eyes. I take a moment to regroup.

"Anyway," I begin again, "to complete the ruse, I have to rob him, right? So I grab his wallet out of his jacket pocket and shove it in my pants." I gaze in Rick's direction as I say, "Stole the pack of cigs I found there, too." A sound akin to a chuckle but not quite squeaks out. "That seems accurate, right? Punk-ass kid would steal his smokes." I shake my head, shuffling my thoughts into place and continue.

"After I'm done with him and the car, I jog back to my apartment. I thought I would be all freaked out, trippin' on adrenaline and shit, but I came home, stripped off my sweaty clothes and passed out. This morning, I got up, put my sweaty clothes back on, stiff but dry, loaded the laundry and the last of my stuff into the car, took my final exam and drove here."

1:19 p.m.

On the stereo, *Cream* begins to play again. Desperate for a distraction, I'm the only one who notices as Prince croons about me being so cool. How everything I do is success. Right. Shit.

All eyes are on me. All brain functions are trying to chew through the big meaty tale I have just put on their plates. They are hungry for it, mentally tearing through it, bit by bit. I wait, sighing, decompressing.

Rick is the first to hit bone. "Nope. I'm trying, man, but no fucking way," he states, shaking his head without ever taking his eyes off me. "Bullshit." Then, "Prove it."

They all nod, not quite in unison, but close enough to be comical. A series of confused bobbleheads.

"Yeah," says Freddy a la Bill Clinton as he mugs a distracted smile and raises a thumb in my direction. "Prove it."

And I do.

I pull a black leather wallet from my back left pocket and toss it on the bed between Rick and Freddy. It bounces heavy on the covers, flopping open and shut and open again like the mouth of a puppet. It is worn smooth and shiny, the way good leather ages. Rick picks it up hesitantly, closes it, flips it open again. Still unsure, he grabs for the cash inside and counts it out. "Two hundred and seventy-three dollars? Holy shit."

"And not a buck to spare," I say as I shake my head, neglecting to mention the four bucks I blew on designer coffee.

Rick removes the driver's license and says, "Mr. Robert Cunningham, you cheapskate bastard, way to go and get yourself killed, ha!" He's flushed and giggly and I grimace at his tone. Then he riffles through the credit cards, grunting satisfaction at every AmEx and Diner's Club he comes across. Even though it appears that I have killed one of his own, I think he appreciates the thinning of the herd.

Stoney picks up the pictures that Rick has tossed aside and fumbles through them. His hands are trembling. He finds a family photo. It is professionally taken, posed and airbrushed. There stands Mister Robert Cunningham and the Missus positioned perfectly behind two tow-headed children around the ages of seven and nine. No one is touching, not husband to wife, not parents to children. Stoney looks at me with incredulity, like he never realized I had two heads. Or a third eye. Or the capacity for murder.

I return his gaze with a grimace and a shrug. Then he finds the nudie pic of some hot, young blonde making a sex face for the camera. This one is not professional and has not been airbrushed. I imagine there was plenty of touching, though. I shrug again and it grows into a full body shudder. I am chilled despite how hot it is in here.

Famous Freddy is freaking out over all of this. He is going through voices faster than MTV goes through pop tarts. "Don't have a cow, man." Bart Simpson. "I'm having a cow, man!" Richard Simmons.

Finally, it's Stoney that asks what this has to do with the club. I think what he really wants to know is why I told them this story. Why I've made them accomplices. *Why, indeed?*

Interdependence? Leverage? Analysis of contextual conditions? I may have a problem...

"I'm not really sure," I tell them, and I mean it. I'm much calmer now. Spent.

Maybe I did know, maybe the antagonistic part of me was poking the beast. Maybe I am the beast and I was poking back. Or maybe I planted a seed just to see how it would grow. *If* it would grow. I honestly don't know.

It grew.

"No fucking way," Rick says, but this time his voice is flush with admiration. Then his eyes get all big and round and the whites match the glow of the light bulb flashing over his head. He shrieks, "I know why you told us! I know!" He jumps around on all fours, tangling the bed covers, dislodging porn and almost Freddy. "I know! This is a special club, man, a really, really fucking special club. No, wait," he pauses in his jubilation to clarify. "Gang. It's a really, really fucking special gang."

"Really, really?" asks Stoney, faux serious, arms crossed, head tilted.

Ignoring him, Rick continues, "You have to kill someone to get in the gang." Rick is so excited, he's practically salivating. "We all have to kill someone, well, except for you," he gives me a cursory glance. "You're good," he says.

Funny, I don't feel good.

Rick clarifies, "You have to kill someone to be a member of the gang, that's the initiation. Oh, and you have to take their pocket money," he adds. Thinking it over quickly, he says, "But just the money, not credit cards or lottery tickets, nothing traceable." He flicks the mess of plastic and pictures, chastising my unprofessionalism.

1:24 p.m.

"Oh my god, this is incredible!" Rick says, focusing on me. He's scrutinizing, assessing, no—reassessing his opinion. "Who'd have thought," he says, shaking his head with a *tsk* and a furrowed brow, "that *you'd* be our first member?"

Honestly, that's the first time I felt my heart and my balls meet in my gut like a mutant organ. Even after everything, his words made me sick to my stomach. "First member" echoes in my head. I swallow, even though I've no saliva to swallow with, and wonder, not for the first and definitely not for the last time, why I shared my story.

Stoney and Freddy are not exactly supportive. Which is a big, fat *duh*, considering this is crazy. Almost, though, which is scary. I'm pretty sure murder has to be a total commitment, so I'm not too worried. Yet.

Then I remember the dickhead driver this morning and how easily I could have accelerated into his Toyota Supra, obliterating his assholey life.

They seem hesitant, even in the face of Rick's pure jubilation. Of course they are hesitant. This is madness. Complete insanity. Rick is all over the idea, need I say more? We are grown men, *ha!* oversized boys, but legal adults all the same. Grown men discussing the idea of killing strangers, and stealing their pocket money, for initiation into a made up club. Gang. Whatever.

Nevermind if I have already completed the task. Nevermind if I may already be crazy. Psychotic. I am my own case study.

I watch the faces of these friends that I have known the longest in my life and I wonder how well we know each other at all.

1:37 p.m.

Rick was the first of this trio to befriend me. Richard
William Covington Harris IV, but we've always just called
him Rick, thank god. To his face anyway. Although I totally
anticipate him getting to a point in his life where he prefers
to be called by his birth name, or at least a part of it,
something more stately. RWC? Harry the Fourth? Covey? I
sense him succumbing to trends, or at least pandering to the
rich and powerful masses. I mean, if his dad should pass
away and he should come into the inheritance, I can totally
see him having them write the check out to Richard, or
Richard William, or King Richard, any name other than
Rick.

But I have to say, as the new kid at yet another new
school, Rick was the first classmate to not only acknowledge
me, but to genuinely seem to enjoy my company.

I met Kevin Stoneham when I was thirteen and my mom
and I moved into the apartment across the hall from his
family. I don't remember ever calling him Kevin, that seems
to be reserved for authority figures, teachers and coaches. Or
his mother when he's in trouble and his father when he's
been a disappointment. Not that either of those happen often.
He gets away with a nickname like Stoney because he's a
stand-up guy. People trust him, he's a nice person, and you
want to be his friend. Lots of people over the years have tried

73

to link his nickname to drug use, but honestly, I've never seen him do drugs. Not even in our high school heyday. Not even as part of the Psychedelic Fours.

With all of the moves my mom and I made, pretty much once a year, I always lived within a few blocks of Stoney, even after his family bought a small house where they still reside. They're the poster family for blue collar. Work hard, play hard, pray hard. Come to think about it, Stoney's family is the opposite of any family I've ever claimed. Maybe that's why I'm so drawn to him. Perhaps he offers the stability I didn't know I desired.

Freddy Stevens came to us through Stoney. They met at some church youth group or YMCA kids' camp around fifth grade. Freddy is what we used to call a 'Klassic Klingon'. I mentally shake my head as I correct myself, *used to?* That he is here today proves he still has Klingon tendencies. Freddy is like that, clinging on, like a burr on your pant cuff. I always think of that kid's book by Dr. Seuss, *Marvin K. Mooney Will You Please Go Now!* He's the kid who lacks the social skills to know when his time has played out, when to contribute or when to shut-up, when to just *go now.* Stoney put up with him when no one else would. He does kind of grow on you, like a fungus. As Freddy would say in his best Gilligan. "I'm a fungi!" I'm calmer and a smile emerges as I hear his voice, one of his voices, in my head.

I watch the faces of these friends and I imagine the thoughts they are struggling with. Deep thoughts, contemplative thoughts, crazy thoughts. And then, with a smirk, I realize I am probably giving them too much credit.

I see a glimmer in Stoney's eyes, a glimmer I can't read. And then he says, "I'm in."

74

1:59 p.m.

I feel the muscles of my knees resign like I'd fall if I was standing and I'm very glad I'm not. "What?" I ask. *No way*, my inner voice screams. *It's a joke, must be a joke.* Just not a funny joke.

After the three of us pick our jaws up off the floor; even Rick could not believe his ears, we stand at attention, waiting. We all thought Stoney would be the hard sell, the hold-out. The one with the most affiliative characteristics. The one with a sense of humanity. Heck, sanity.

Of course, then Freddy has to jump in. He announces himself as Rod Roddy from *The Price is Right*, speaking into his hand like it's a microphone. "Freddy Stevens, come on down! You're the next contestant on *Murder Gang Initiation!*" He stands up, waving his hands in the air, high-fiving invisible members of the live studio audience and running around the massive bed. He makes crowd sounds into his cupped hands.

Murder Gang Initiation. Like it's a game. Nice.

Rick is dancing on the bed. Jumping high enough to clip the ceiling fan with his fist.

The ceiling fan, I contemplate, *why isn't it on?*

But the thought is gone just as quickly as Rick hops to the floor and says with a clap, "We have to make some rules.

We have to have a plan." Mr. Authority, he says, "We can't just go around killing willy-nilly."

"Willy-nilly?" I wonder aloud. I roll my eyes and add under my breath, "What the fuck?"

2:01 p.m.

Murder preparation is hungry business, so we order pizza and move the planning party outside.

Rick's family inherited an amazing estate. There are sprawling grounds, a wooded area, and beautiful gardens with a fountain containing a topless mermaid spilling water in the pond from a large lily pad. The things we used to fantasize about that mermaid, ooh boy, I tell ya'. With hindsight, she may be the root cause of Rick's porn addiction.

There're also tennis courts, a sand pit for volleyball which is currently netless and mostly pit, and a kidney shaped pool with guest house.

Michelle is still on deck, shimmering from a quick dip to cool off. Risky business, if you ask me. The water seems more au natural than chlorinated. Wouldn't doubt it if their mom took the pool boy, too. Michelle's wet hair hangs in strings across her shoulders and she's wearing sunglasses that cover half her face. Up close, her boniness and angles are even more pronounced. *Wait*, I think, *are those bruises?* I offer a half-hearted hello to her as again I ask in a hushed voice, "What's up with Michelle?"

Rick shoots me a dirty look and tells me to leave his sister alone.

We head to the pool house, a handy little abode with one generous bedroom, a full bath, and a large open great room that includes a living area with a fireplace, wet bar, and entertainment center. There's a full kitchen along the wall and a long table with several chairs. For whatever reason, it's actually cooler in here and for the first time in hours, I do not feel oppressed by the stickiness of the day. Despite the color of the pool, it smells like chlorine in here. I like that; fresh, summery, nostalgic.

Upon entering, three of us head towards the living room, while Rick goes straight to the kitchen. He's rummaging through drawers and slamming cupboard doors until finally we hear a victorious, "Ta-da!" as he finds a spiral notebook and pencil. When he turns to set them on the table, he notices that we are not there with him. Crushed at first, he recovers quickly with a, "Hellooo, over here."

We reluctantly amble over to the table and sit down on the heavy dark mahogany chairs, not as cushy as the sectional, that's for sure. As Rick is getting situated at the head of the table, his sister screams to us that the pizza guy is here and if we think she's paying for it, well, we can suck…We lose the rest of the threat in the screech of wooden chairs scraping the imported Italian tile floor. While Rick is bringing in the pizza, Stoney goes to the fridge. It's pretty sparsely stocked with only a few bottles of beer and cans of pop. He grabs the cans and starts passing them out.

"I'll have a Coke," I say. I always have Coke. Not Tab, not RC Cola, not Mountain Dew, and never Pepsi. I'd rather go thirsty than drink Pepsi.

Stoney looks at me and rolls his eyes. "Really," he says, "Coke? I never knew."

Rick sets down the pizza and Stoney tosses him a Coke. Rick catches it, looks and says, "Coke? C'mon guys, it's Happy Hour!" as he tosses it back. Stoney catches and immediately releases, sending it back to Rick.

"I'd wait to open that," Stoney says, closing the refrigerator door and sitting down.

Rick is just standing there, mouth agape, arms out at his sides, holding a potentially explosive can of pop in one hand.

"Excuse me, my friends, but this is not a Coke drinking event. Toss me a cold beer, would ya'?"

Stoney and I make eye contact, brows raised. I shrug, *whatever*, while Stoney does a quick shake of his head, *no*.

Rick sees this, and as he is looking at Stoney squarely in the face, he tosses the can back then reaches into a pocket of his cargo shorts and removes a flask. "Fine, drink your *soda*," he says. He grins, that snarky shit-eating grin that's gotten us into more trouble than we care to remember, and uncaps the canteen before taking a deep swig.

Freddy, who has been playing visual ping-pong, bouncing his attentions between the three of us, adds, "Uh, hey boss, we prolly shouldn't be makin' plans whilse we's under the in-flu-ence."

I'm not sure who he is supposed to be, some sort of mobster lackey, I guess. That is not a reflection of his ability, but more indicative of my being out of the entertainment loop.

"But yous can—"

Rick cuts Freddy's words short with a glance and drags the back of his hand across his mouth. He slips the flask back into his pocket and sits down at the table.

We settle in around the end near Rick and the delectable delivery. Burning the roofs of our mouths on steaming hot stringing cheese, we begin stuffing our face old school style, with no manners. I think it's equal parts a procrastinate measure, *I can't start making murder rules, my mouth is full*, as much as hunger.

For me, it's the latter, I'm starving. And although I'm curious about the "murder rules", I'm not really invested. I don't need no stinkin' rules. Murder anarchy, that was my thing. Snorting on my hilarity, I nearly choke to death on a mouthful of 'za.

"What the fuck," Stoney shouts, backing away from my sputtered pizza spray.

"Sorry, dude," I say, wiping away a smile and greasy remnants. *Murder anarchy*. What can say? I crack me up.

After a while, Rick slouches back in his chair, pooching out his soft belly and giving it a contented pat. "Okay, boys, let's get down to business." A burp escapes, grows into a belchy verbal exhalation, and then a robust laugh. He sits up, grabs the notebook, Mr. Professional. If he had a time card, he'd be punching it in the machine. It may be me, but I think there is a cumulative sigh of resignation as Stoney, Freddy, and I adjust ourselves forward at the table.

The buzz generated from the telling of my story has passed. How quickly we acclimate. Not even an hour ago I told these three childhood friends that I'd committed a murder. Now, it's no big deal. Oh? That killing thing? Gees, that was ages ago. We're all past that. Well, not all. Not Rick. He's scribbling furiously, I have no idea what, but he's on a roll and he's not going to let our hesitancy slow him down.

Letting out a victorious *whoop!*, he stops writing and looks at us. His cheeks are flushed. He's absolutely glowing at the prospect of starting his own club and passing initiation.

I should have said *STOP! This is insane. You can't be serious—we can't do this.* But I don't think I thought we really would. And besides, "should have" is the bastard child of hindsight, a cruel and tortuous joker.

Rick reads us what he's written. It's all formal and shit with lots of whereins and heretofores. Seriously, if he had put one whit of this effort into any of the schools he attended, he'd have a doctorate by now. Or at least a passing grade.

He's so excited, he's out of breath. His smile is so wide, it affects the annunciation of his words. I've seen him high a big fat handful of times. Once, at some party a few years ago, he was hopped up on hoop. Or gopped up on goop? My grandma used to say something like that. Anyway, he was experimenting with crack at the time. That was sedate compared to this. Under different circumstances, this would inspire a good time. Under different circumstances, this would be a Rick we'd all enjoy.

He clears his throat and continues reading what he's written. Seems he's banged out the preamble and it's time for the body. The rules. The actual fucking rules for initiation into a club that we made up. A killing club. I'm sorry, I keep forgetting. A killing *gang*.

I recall Freddy's earlier announcement in my head. *Freddy Stevens, come on down, you're the next contestant on Murder Gang Initiation!* I hear his crowd cheers and see him high-fiving the live studio audience and wonder how far off

81

this vision actually is. I wonder what kind of sponsors you'd get for a show like that?

Murder Gang Initiation.

Too much, man, too much.

2:37 p.m.

"Okay, okay." Rick takes a deep breath, preparing himself for the business ahead. "So, rule number one…"

He is interrupted by a calm voice that is vaguely familiar.

"Master Yoshi's first rule was, 'Possess the right thinking. Only then can one receive the gifts of strength, knowledge, and peace.'" Freddy presses his palms together and bows his head.

"What the hell?" Rick is not amused.

I concentrate, repeating the words and voice in my head. Stoney leans over and whispers, "Master Splinter."

My face lights up with recollection. Teenage Mutant Ninja Turtles, of course! I shout the words, "Heroes in a half-shell, turtle power!"

Rick shoots us a nasty glance and continues, "We're doing this today. Boom. If we don't, we won't. Know what I'm saying?" We nod. "After midnight is okay, I'm not sure how long it will take and we've got three to do." He makes eye contact all around, *you with me?* his gaze asks. He receives silent stares in return. Consent. "Okay, next. Rule number two, it can't be anyone you know."

He's still writing when Stoney, I swear to god he does this, raises his hand. He raises his fucking hand! Before Rick can look up from the notebook, Stoney says, "I disagree with that rule."

Utter disbelief is reflected in Rick's amazed expression. He stops mid-written word and says, "Huh?"

Stoney falters, but just a little. "Um, I don't think that should be a rule is all. I mean," he takes a breath as he's trying to recoup. "I'm not saying we can kill our parents or our friends, but come on, it's a small town, we're in a time crunch, it could happen." He's on a roll now, gaining momentum and confidence. "I'm just saying, what if you kill someone, find out you know them, and then have to kill someone *else* just to have it count? See?"

"Fine, fine." Rick doesn't like it, but he frantically erases rule number two, griping under his breath about old erasers sucking. "Okay, what's rule number two then?"

"Like you said before, Rick," Stoney says, "kill them, take their pocket money. But that's all, remember? No wallets or credit cards."

"And no purses," Rick adds.

"Um, okay." Stoney seems to ponder this but then continues. "And no possessions. No car keys, lottery tickets, photos, etcetera. Nothing but money, right? Cash and loose change. Sound good?"

"All right, all right," Rick replies. "Slow down!" He's again writing as fast as he can, the lead scrawling across the paper. He balks, pencil hovering. "Loose change? Seriously?"

Stoney raises and drops his shoulders. "Whatever. Pocket money."

There is silence at the table, Stoney and I look at each other warily. I imagine alarm bells are going off behind his eyes, too, yet no one interrupts the madness. Maybe only I hear the warning sirens?

"What else?" Rick asks. "Come on, we've got to have at least three rules. It's murder for chrissakes."

"Rule number three," I say, my first contribution since telling my tale, "each crime must be committed individually. No assistance. No *accomplice*," I amend, accentuating the word.

"And you've got to prove it!" Rick nearly screams.

"What? You want to witness? To watch?" asks Stoney. "That's just creepy, man."

"Yes, er, no, but how can you prove you did it? I mean, it would be easier is all I'm saying. You, know, if we saw it."

"We'll be together," I say. "And besides, if you don't want to, don't. Nothing to prove then. Let's stop now." *Yes*, I think, *stop now*. You all win, I never thought it'd go this far. This is as close as I get to calling it quits, but it's not like I get up and walk out. I look around, searching each pair of eyes for a weakness, some hesitancy, something I can use. I get nothing.

Stoney stretches, rocking back in his chair and says, "If we're all on board, then why would we lie about it anyway?"

"Well, sirs, he didn't have a witness." It comes from Freddy but sounds like Bond, James Bond. Connery Bond.

They all look at me. I raise my eyebrows, *so?*

"Yeah, yeah," Rick says with a dismissive roll of his eyes. "But he started the whole thing. He didn't have any rules."

Murder anarchy.

"Don't you believe him? I believe him. We wouldn't be here if we didn't believe him."

85

I am sick to my stomach. Ill. The pizza that I wolfed down sits in my gut like fresh cement. Wet. Sodden. Heavy. Like the guilt that it is. *Stop this, stop it right now!* I scream on the inside. But on the outside, I just sit there. I know on some sick level I am curious. Would this happen? Could this happen? I wonder what my motivation is. I mean, my earlier actions were purely reflexive, but this, this is different. Is this an example of intrinsic motivation, or extrinsic?

Then I say, "This is crazy. What are the chances of four guys committing four murders and no one getting caught?" My voice is loud as I speak over the *whoop, whoop* of the warning bells in my head.

There is an awkward silence that ripples around the table. Glances are exchanged as fingers drum on the gnarled wood table and feet shuffle beneath it.

"We can do it," Rick says quietly, no longer making eye contact.

I realize that he's thinking it's not fair if I got to kill someone and he doesn't.

"Think about how many assholes deserve to die? It's a public service, really."

Fuckin' Supra-man.

"We are smart and we are dedicated and besides, if you get caught, you're obviously not in the gang," Rick finishes.

A giggle unintentionally bubbles up from my throat. Smiles break out around the table. "Well, duh. Obviously."

"There's your rule number four," Stoney says.

"Wait! What about rule number three? We didn't finish three."

"How about, witnesses are encouraged but not necessary? I mean, once again, we don't really know what

86

we're doing. Maybe an opportunity comes, like mine," I add, "that you can't miss waiting for your clubmates to arrive, you know?"

Nodding, "Yeah, fine, okay," says Rick. "But do not call us clubmates. We're...what are we? Brothers?"

"Ganstahs, mutha fuckahs!" shouts a throaty voiced Freddy.

Once again there is laughter and everyone seems to relax a little. I no longer feel my pizza, although that sense of culpability till prods.

"Let me read what we've got so far," Rick says. Clearing his throat, he summarizes, "Rule number one, the initiation must take place today. Number two, only pocket money counts. Rule number three, you must work individually, and four is about getting caught...or not getting caught. Number four is not really a rule," Rick decides in all seriousness. "How about if that's addressed in the conclusion of the doctrine?"

Eyebrows rise, word mouthed in unison, *doctrine?*

"Hey, I say, I say fellas," it's Jimmy Stewart. "Uh, fellas, what's the name of our gang? Uh, we know what kind of club it's no-o-ot." Freddy smiles. "But what's it called?"

"And what's the purpose of the pocket money?" Stoney enquires. "I mean, what's the point?"

There is mutual pondering as we try and decide what the purpose is, what's the point, what *is* this gang?

Rick's chair grunts on the tile as he jumps out of his seat. "Oh! How about a little extra incentive?" Eyes wide, he looks expectantly around the table.

"Like the pleasure of killing is not incentive enough?" Stoney snorts.

Rick shoots Stoney an offended look and says, "Not funny."

Because joking about murder is off limits.

"Yeah," Freddy says as Barney Rubble. "How about whoever collects the most pocket money gets to keep all of the money? Sounds yabba dabba moneylicious to me!" He finishes with a Barney chuckle, "Uh, uh, uh."

Rick stares at him, his glare a yin-yang of loaded daggers fused with don't waste my time. *Poor pathetic kid,* his smirk says, emphasis on poor. Or maybe he just really doesn't like the Flintstones. Nope, probably the poor thing.

Under his breath, Freddy says something about what makes Rick think he'll win. I can't tell who he is using to channel the message, it's muffled and he turns his head away.

Rick shoves the table into Freddy's t-shirted chest and in a low voice growls, "Who says I won't?"

"Boys...guys...clubmates." I snicker. "Settle down. What do you propose Rick, what's the prize?"

"Hmmm, I dunno," he says, but I think he does. He's pretending to consider, complete with finger tap to the temple. "Or do I?" Then he says, "I know!" but I hear *Eureka!* as his tapping finger suddenly points straight up in the air. God, these guys crack me up.

"The pocket money," he states matter-of-factly, "decides who gets to decide. If you collect the most pocket money, you not only get to be president—"

"Read my lips, no new taxes," Freddy interjects as George Bush.

Rick presses the table again, slowly this time. I believe if he had it his way, he would bisect Freddy one crushed rib at a time.

"Uh, I don't think gangs have presidents," Stoney says, holding tightly to the table to keep it from further action.

"CEO's?" I ask innocently.

"Shut up. Leader, okay? Most pocket money earns you the title of Gang Leader," Rick says. "And, if you get the most pocket money, as leader, you get to decide what the gang is called."

He looks around, obviously proud of this idea. "What do you think? Sound fair?"

Freddy stands up so fast, his chair wobbles and he sits back down again, hard. Absently rubbing his bruised chest, he is alert and at attention. He likes this idea. Suddenly he is *all* in. Better than money is power. Who needs some extra cash to stick in his paltry Velcro wallet when there is the opportunity to be boss. And not just any boss, oh no, *Rick's boss*. He is all over this new prize like scum on bong water.

"Sounds good," I say. "My take was $273. Beat that."

"Okay," Rick says. "Let me finish writing this all out and then we can sign at the bottom. You know, to make it official."

"Do you think that's a good idea?" asks Stoney. "Do you really want to have written proof that we agreed to commit murder? What if something goes wrong?"

Rick looks wounded. And confused.

Stoney takes a deep breath, exhales slowly. "What if, say in thirty years, you wake up one morning hating me and want revenge for some reason? It's dangerous, man. And stupid."

I can tell by the developing look on Rick's face that Stoney had him until the 'stupid' part. That's all it took to flip his pissed-off switch. After all the valid points that Stoney made, all Rick heard was, "you're stupid."

Immediately defensive, Rick motions to the notebook scribbles and asks, "What was the point of all this then?"

"So we don't go around killing willy-nilly," I say with utmost seriousness, which is good because no one laughs. I try again, "It's okay, Rick. We all know the rules. We all agree to the rules. We are familiar with the introduction and conclusion of the doctrine, so let's sign it. Then burn it, okay? Something binding and symbolic."

"Perfect," says Stoney.

An energetic, "Amen," from preacher Freddy.

Scribble, scribble, signature, dot. Passed around the table, precursory perusal, signed by all. Rick fishes in one of his pockets for the lighter. *Don't leave home without it*, the bad boy scout's steadfast rule. We each hold a corner as he places the flame beneath the page and burns from the center out. Our fingers release when the flames begin licking uncomfortably close. Rick smacks at the last of the glowing embers that have fallen on his parent's mahogany table. Not even a blemish. I imagine this table has seen far worse in the last twenty years and survived. I admire what real money can buy.

3:10 p.m.

Once again, we sit around staring at each other. *Now what?*

"Celebratory smoke?" Rick asks me.

I nod and he lights two at once before passing one over. I don't know how I feel about the celebratory part, there's nothing about this day worth celebrating, but I inhale deeply and feel the menthol fill my lungs. It's a bad habit and one that I really can't afford. I admit it; I'm a smoke bum, as in "can I bum a smoke?" I consider it co-dependency at its best, a constructive reciprocation. Most smokers eagerly comply, aware that social smoking is more publicly acceptable.

The afternoon heat has found its way into the pool house and I'm ready to move on.

"Who's first?" Rick asks.

"You?" I wonder aloud.

"Oh, no," he sneers. "No, no. I'll be last, I think. I'm working on a plan. Plus," he shoots a look in Freddy's direction, "I'll need to know how much pocket money you losers find."

Find. Interesting choice of words.

"I'll go," says Stoney.

Bewildered is an understatement. Again I feel faint, that mutant organ having hijacked my blood flow pulses hot in my belly. "Really?" I ask, choking on my exhale.

"Yeah," he says. Then, "Come on, guys." He rises casually from the table, collecting his pizza mess and shoving it into the overflowing trash can on his way out the door.

Michelle is no longer by the pool. She has either disintegrated into a pile of ash, or she's retreated inside for some quality daytime television viewing. It's definitely hotter now than it was when we entered the pool house. It doesn't seem like any of the humidity has burned off, though.

I break into a sweat just walking to Stoney's car. Of course, it's his car we'll take. Not only has he volunteered to go first, *second?*, but it's a sensible four-door sedan that, although cheap by comparison, will give us the most room.

Rick has a sporty import convertible that is impressive, but completely useless. And I'm not sure, but I think Freddy came on his bike, as in bicycle.

My two-door hatchback piece of crap that barely fits me is already full. For a moment, I genuinely consider asking Rick if I can use his machines. The laundry is already detergented, it would only take a minute it throw it in. Heck, I'd even do some of his. I shudder involuntarily at the idea of touching his unmentionables. *Nevermind*, I think that's more trade than it's worth.

"No smoking," Stoney says.

Rick and I both drag deeply before flicking our butts onto the gravel drive. We laugh at the synchronicity of it.

"Been practicing," we say in unison.

"Jinx, you owe me a Coke," I interject quickly and everybody laughs. Hard to believe we are on our merry way to murder.

Of course Rick gets shotgun with me and Freddy shoehorning in the back.

I open the car door to slide in behind Rick and am shocked to see a car seat in my space. "Uh, Stoney?"

"Oh, yeah. Yeah." He comes around the car and moves me out of the way. Fiddling with the clasp, he drags the seat out. "Pop the trunk," he says.

I do, holding it open while he sets the chair inside, struggling to fit it in amongst other miscellaneous baby stuff.

"Stoney?"

He slams the trunk, dusting off his hands and says, "Told you, things change."

Rick waits until the three of us are settled to say, "Hold up, Stone, I gotta piss." He runs past the building we just exited to the main house, up the front steps, and disappears behind the heavy doors.

"What's up with that?" I ask. "He could've gone in the pool house."

Freddy laughs and in the radio voice of Paul Harvey, says, "Rick Harris, he could've pissed in the pool house bathroom, he could've peed in the yard, he could've drained his lizard from the seat of the car into the dusty gravel drive. But Rick Harris suffers from…a potty complex. And that's the rest of the story."

"Ha," says Stoney, "remember that time he was peeing in the school parking lot? What was it? Some sort of anti-establishment commentary?"

"Pre-potty complex," Paul Harvey offers.

"Naw," I say. "He was just too lazy to go back inside."

"Whatever," Stoney continues, "he was peeing and somebody saw him and honked, causing him to pee on his own car."

"The root of his potty complex," Paul Harvey concludes.

"He was so pissed!" I say.

"How, ah, pissed was he?" offers Gene Rayburn from *Match Game*.

"He was so pissed," I begin, but Stoney interrupts.

"He was so pissed that he peed on every car he could reach until he ran out of stream."

"Marking his territory."

"Pretty clever, actually," Stoney says. "Making the best of a bad situation." We all nod, good ole Rick, leading his troops by piss and pride.

We're mentally reminiscing about high school parking lots when Rick comes out. He dashes down the stairs clutching his abdomen.

"You okay?" I ask, as he slides into the shotgun seat.

"Yep." He leans forward, fumbles on the floor then comes up with a pack of Doublemint gum. Offering it over his shoulder, he says, "Double your pleasure, dude?"

I take a stick and put it in my pocket. "Uh, thanks."

"Okay, let's hit it!" Rick says, bouncing his palms off the dashboard.

The car is steamy despite having the windows open. Or maybe because of it. Stoney cranks the a/c and we roll the windows up only after the cold air starts blowing. His radio is tuned to NPR, talk radio. I hate talk radio. I enjoy the general distraction of music. Talk makes me listen, and listening makes me think, and quite frankly, I think enough already.

I wait the duration of the driveway and two full blocks before I state what I consider must be the obvious. "You have a kid?"

"I do."

94

"And…" And so many things! "D'you get married?"

Rick sniggers from the passenger seat and turns so he's not looking at Stoney.

"Nope."

"C'mon, man, catch me up." I don't know why he doesn't want to tell me, I mean, shit, he's a father. That's huge!

Freddy begins singing in the pitch perfect tone of Barry Manilow. "Ohm Andi, you came and—"

"She came all right." Rick cracks himself up.

Freddy croons the next lyric. He really does have an amazing voice. "And I need you today, ohm Andi."

Stoney exhales deeply and sinks a little deeper in the bucket seat. His hands slide down from ten and two o'clock and settle at the bottom of the steering wheel. "Yes, I have a kid. No, I am not married. Yes, Bailey was…unplanned." He pauses, hitting the indicator before switching lanes. "Andi and I," he releases a breath and shakes his head before continuing. "We don't love each other, but we do love the baby. She's almost six months old."

It sounds rehearsed to me. I feel like he's been telling himself these words for so long, six months at least, they're rote. I lean forward and tag his shoulder. "Congratulations, man. I think it's cool. You'll be an awesome dad."

There's no sound in the car except for the murmur of the low radio and occasional blowing of the fans. I'm kind of obsessed with the idea that Stoney has a kid. A kid! How did that happen? No, I know *how* it happened; I know where babies come from. It's just, wow, I can't believe Stoney would be so careless. I can see one of the other of us, well, no, really only Rick, getting hit with an unplanned

95

pregnancy, and I have to say, that baby is really lucky it wasn't him.

"Dude!"

"Huh?" I say, startled from my kid-think. "What?"

"I just asked if you were seeing anyone." Stoney says. "You dating?"

"Dating? How archaic," Rick interjects. "Bangin', man, who ya' bangin'?"

"Sorry," Stoney says. "Yes, please tell us if you are banging anyone."

Again Rick interrupts and says, "Bangin' everybody! Am I right?" He turns in his seat to fist bump me and I leave him hanging.

"Naw, I'm good," I tell them. To Stoney, I add, "You know me; I don't like to be involved."

Rick scoffs at my use of the word, 'involved'.

"Not since Donna," Rick says, laughing. "No, wait! Not since Be-e-eth."

Beside me, Freddy breaks into a spot on version of Peter Criss singing that song, *Beth*. I am struck with a sudden melancholy heartache.

I didn't date a lot in high school. Not real keen on relationships, you know. My mom was, how shall I put this delicately? She was not the best role model. Her romantic histories kind of burned me in that department. And if she couldn't figure it out at thirty-something, what made me think I was ready for a girlfriend at sixteen?

The one girl I thought I loved, despite all of my actions to the contrary, was Beth Johnson. Sweet Beth. I could hear her calling! But I couldn't come home right now. The voice in my head sounds identical to the one singing beside me in the back of Stoney's car. I loved that song. Bought the KISS album for that one track, pretty much wore the grooves straight through. I'd listen to it for hours.

She broke my heart and I've always said, that was just as well. I'm not the kind of guy who should be in a relationship. I bring bad mojo to the table. I don't exactly come from a long line of committed people. I don't know my bio dad. And my mom, well, she's got more baggage than a 747. That's not all, of course. There's also the whole *I seem to lose people I love* thing. There's only so much a young heart can handle.

"Stop!" Rick demands, slamming his palms on the dashboard. The car jerks slightly as Stoney reacts to the order, but then he continues on. He is a man on a mission.

"Not the car," Rick blurts. "The song."

Freddy stops mid-chorus and I'll be honest, a little bit I feel gypped.

"Remember that other girl you dated?" Rick laughs and of course we all know exactly which other girl he's referencing.

That would be Carol. She had the biggest boobs I've ever seen in person. You know all those nicknames they give tits? Like hooters, ta-tas, and melons? Carol's photo may very well have accompanied the definition for every one of those terms in the adolescent slang dictionary.

We only went out a couple of times. I never even asked her to go with me or anything, but a lot of guys, present company included, were really jealous that I got to come in contact with those jugs. I didn't, really, but that's nobody's business. I think Carol liked me because I was cool about them. Like, I liked her, you know? She was nice and smart and pretty funny. Truth is, they scared me. I was at the height of my uncontrollable boner phase, what we use to call our "growth spurt". Anyway, I feigned respect in order to not have to navigate the wetlands of embarrassment.

When I didn't immediately try to cop a feel at the movie theater, she actually offered them up later, on our third date. She'd never been "rejected" before and although it's what she said she wanted, I think even she thought she was nothing if not for her boobs. By our fourth date, she was confiding in me how she wanted to have a reduction. She had it all planned out, you know for medical purposes and stuff. She was going to hurt her back. Not much of a stretch considering how sore she usually was from lugging those things around all day, but she had to make it real enough, and serious enough, that her parents, and especially the insurance company, would allow it.

I remember being in her room making out and all of a sudden her shirt and bra were off. Don't get too excited for me, it truly wasn't like that. Next thing I know, she's standing against the bedroom wall, pressing her naked breasts to her chest with flayed hands and asking me if that doesn't look better. More natural. I couldn't be trusted to speak, so I just nodded.

Better? Not exactly. It looked like she had flesh colored dinner plates squashed to her chest. That's how she got the nickname—

"Corelle!" Rick shouts.

I never should have shared that story. And I still wonder how Rick knows about Corelle, the poor man's china.

Rick seems to really be enjoying my brief dating history. "Man, she had the best rack." He turns to face the back again. "Ran into her a couple of months ago at the mall. She had the reduction. I swear, I didn't even recognize her. And suffice it to say, it was less than a pleasure when she hugged me. He shakes his head. "Such a shame." Turning back to face the front, he elbows Stoney. "I bet Andi has nice tits."

"Shut up."

And again, I'm back to the fact that Stoney is a dad. Andi is now the mother of his child, her tits are absolutely off limits.

"Are we there yet?" Freddy whines in the voice of every kid stuck in the back seat on their way anywhere.

"Close," Stoney replies.

Since it's obvious he has a target, I entertain ideas of who he might be offing. Some dick from the gym that double parks his Ram truck and has bull testicles hanging from the boat hitch? That'd be interesting, but no, sounds too confrontational.

Some asshole customer? I imagine that'd be quite a list, retail sucks. How would he narrow it down? Who could it be? I can't imagine he has an enemy. I keep thinking, racking my brain for the Stoney I knew while at the same time I'm realizing that this is a Stoney I don't know. *Things change*, he said. He wasn't kidding.

We approach Cleaver's Family Market and I wonder if it's his boss. Naw, I'm pretty sure the manager is a woman, with a purse! I also think she's a pretty good boss, as far as bosses go. Considering he's been there nearly eight years, I can't imagine she's pocket money murder worthy. Interesting that he pushed for it to be okay to be someone you know.

I look out the window as familiar places go by. Once again I am slapped by a sense of nostalgia. The four of us, cruising through town together…late nights, loud music, laughing and shit. We did have some good times.

Freddy is antsy. Sitting beside me in the back, the whole bench seat shakes with his twitching, bouncing and tapping. He is excited to be part of this, crazy as this is. He is eager to prove himself. He can't wait to kick Rick's ass. I smile at his enthusiasm, and you know? I wish him well. Rick needs a good ass-kicking and it would mean so much more, to all of us, if it came from Freddy.

Rick senses the energy in the car. He must nip that. This is his show. He starts laughing, slapping a knee.

"Remember that time when we rolled the Porsche into the lamp post?" Laughing harder, this memory is a hoot.

"Right," says Stoney, "because you thought you knew how to drive. You didn't."

"Ha," Rick says, levity still strong in his voice. "I was twelve, how was I supposed to know that N stood for Neutral? What the fuck does neutral even mean?"

"It means your driveway is steep. Ahhhhh!" Freddy screams like Sam Kinison.

"Come on," Rick says, humor abating. "It just made sense. If D is for Drive, then N means *Not* driving.

"It's cool," I say between snorts of laughter, "you were *not driving*, that's for sure."

The car fills with the hilarity of three. I think Rick regrets his contribution to our travels down memory lane.

"I got one," Stoney says, his words sputtering between chuckles. "How about the time we snuck out at midnight to make a Taco Bell run and ran out of gas?"

100

"Taco Bell is three times better! Fitty-nine, seventy-nine, niney-nine," Freddy sings.

"We walked home empty-handed, I might add. And I loved me some Taco Bell." But wait, it gets funnier. "And then—" I pause, taking a couple of deep breaths. "Your dad called the cops and reported the car stolen. And we let him!"

"Did you ever tell him?" Stoney asks. "Did he find out?"

With a forced smile, Rick says, "Yeah, I think the police told him. They found the car and returned it, still on empty." He shrugs. "You know my dad, no big deal." He sighs. "Nothing was ever a big deal."

I analyze the implications of that statement.

"Okay," Rick says, refreshed and eager to try again. "How about that time we borrowed one of my dad's cars, legit like, to go to the drive-in."

"You mean the time that you reversed into another of your dad's cars?" I ask.

"It was a little funny," Stoney says. "He drove his dad's car *into* his dad's car. Not something you see every day."

"I didn't think it was funny!" interjects Freddy as Barney Fife. He is absently rubbing his left elbow as he speaks. "Made me ride in the trunk!" he cries to Rick. "The other guys got to ride up front. What was that all about?"

Alamo! I meet Stoney's eyes in the rear view mirror. We know what that was all about, what it's always about. Rick is Rick. He's an asshole, always has been. We were just dumb kids along for the ride. Literally. I think about this, and wonder if we're still just dumb kids. Along for another ride.

"Like you had the money to pay for the drive-in." Rick says. "It was a two-seater, man, relax."

"But why," asks Freddy in a voice I don't recognize through gritted teeth, "were we taking a two-seater to the drive-in?"

Good question, Fred, I think.

Ignoring him, Rick continues, "Stoney was straddling the stick shift, one ass cheek on the driver's seat, one ass cheek on the passenger side."

"For real, man, about circumcised myself on the gear shift."

Oh, that's right, I think. Stoney's dick proximity was the problem. Rick was hesitant adjusting the gear and couldn't exactly see if he was in drive or reverse when he hit the gas.

"Do you remember," Freddy asks in a voice unnervingly reminiscent of Hal 9000 from *2001: A Space Odyssey*, "how he slammed one car into the other and the trunk would not open? Do you remember how I was trapped?" That voice comes across passive yet there is an edge to it.

Rick seems to remember just fine as his laughter erupts anew. "Oh yeah," he yells, spinning in the seat as much as the belt will allow. "I forgot about that! Jaws of life! You really wrecked my dad's car."

"Me?" Freddy screams.

I nudge him with my elbow and shake my head. *Don't do it, don't go there.* I relay the message with a pointed stare. "Just chill, Fred," I say. "Seriously, al-a-mo."

Freddy sits back with a huff. His normally pale skin is flushed and all that energy he was exhibiting earlier has turned to anger. A wasted emotion. Wasted with Freddy, wasted on Rick. Rick returns to the captain's position. I can't see his face, but I know there is a wicked grin pasted there. To the victor go the smiles.

3:29 p.m.

Stoney rounds a bend and turns into a narrow alley. For some reason, Rick feels the need to say, "Uh, remember no friends or family."

I smile. Like we devised this whole plan, a plan he actually devised, so we could kill him in some alley. What a twit.

We pull up behind a sad little one car garage, the tires scraping over broken pavement. The sad little garage backs up to a sad little brownstone. The fenced yard is surrounded by a rickety picket fence that could not successfully keep anything in or out. There seems to be more growth between the cracks in the sidewalk than in the patchy lawn. The gutters sag and the door and window frames are weathered and worn. I'm glad it's a brick foundation. That may be the only reason it's still standing.

Stoney is reverent as he exits the car, opens the gate and proceeds up the back steps to the screenless porch door. He reaches under a long dead potted plant and retrieves a key. Shaking off a pesky earwig, he knocks as he unlocks the door and enters with a, "*Hellooo.*"

It is not a question. He knows who lives here and he knows they are home.

We follow him through the back door into a small kitchen. The air hangs heavy with years of home cooking and most recently, microwave popcorn.

"It's me," Stoney calls to the mystery person in the next room. He's shouting to be heard over the blaring television. It's the dramatic exchange of characters on some sappy soap opera. I hear familiar music and recognize *The Young and Restless*. For the few months my mom and I lived with my Gram, we used to watch it with her religiously.

Stoney halts us as he continues walking. Rick starts to follow, but I reach out and mouth the word, *no*. We stay back, out of her sightline. We can see, and maybe hear, hard to tell with the television shrieking. *Witnesses are encouraged but not necessary.*

Who is she? Is he really going to do this? What is he really going to do?

Stoney approaches the frail figure sitting on the side of the davenport and touches her shoulder gently.

She takes a shaky hand and brushes it over his. "Do I have a delivery today?" she asks, looking at him with subtle uncertainty. She is happy to see him, but a bit confused.

"No, Gracie," he says, punching buttons on the remote to pause the VCR. "I'm here for another reason." From the kitchen, we see him hesitate. He looks into her faded eyes, and continues. "That other reason." Stoney's shoulders sag, then stiffen. "That thing we've been talking about."

Gracie gazes at him questioningly. From where I'm standing, it appears she has no idea what he's talking about. I'm sure this makes it harder for him.

"You know," he prods, "the other—" but then he changes course. "You look good today," he whispers.

104

"Oh." She blushes, a sweet circle of color blooming in each of her pale cheeks. "You know, Kevin, I am so tired." She releases a deep breath that leaves her wheezing.

The next time she looks at him, there is a spark there. "Really?" she asks between gasps. With an arthritically curled hand, she touches her hair, fluffing the top and tucking the side behind her ear. "I look good today?" She pauses, her breath catching. "It'll be nice to look good for Frank." She winks, wrinkled lids meet, then open on twinkling blue eyes.

"Are you sure?" Stoney asks, hushed but urgent. He needs to know.

We need to know.

Gracie gazes up. A smile touches the corners of her deeply lined mouth. She nods and moves the bag of popcorn to the end table where it joins several bottles of prescription drugs. She shakes out the afghan, dislodging a few stray kernels, then leans back comfortably. She closes her eyes.

Stoney picks up a lacy, decorative pillow from the sofa and clutches it with both hands. I see his knuckles whiten with the grip. Gracie seems very relaxed. She breathes shallowly, a slight whistle escaping with each exhale. I envy her calm. Death should always come so serenely.

It feels like my heart will beat a path right out of my chest. I can't imagine how Stoney feels.

"It's okay." Stoney's mantra, over and over again. "It's okay, it's okay…"

"Wait!" she says, suddenly alert, startling him, and me. My heart is now pounding a path through my head.

"What?" he cries, dropping the pillow to his side.

"No, no," she says urgently. "Get the pillow from the bed. The one with the blue trim. That was Frank's. Yes, that's the one," she adds with a wistful smile, eyes looking toward the bedroom and beyond.

Stoney exits our range, out of sight. The three of us crouching in the kitchen take the opportunity to silently adjust our positions. Freddy nearly topples the garbage can but rights it with a quick jerk and a Marcel Marceau exclamation.

Gracie jumps at the noise, opens her eyes and stares in the general direction of the television, to the right of where we hunker. She seems so frail, I feel sorry for surprising her. Then I think, if she has a heart attack before Stoney returns with Frank's pillow, will it still count? You know, for the murder club.

What the serious fuck are we doing?

The VCR resumes play at the end of a loud commercial which leads into characters on the show arguing. I wonder if that's really the best thing for her to hear as she's, you know...

I consider sneaking around the corner and turning the TV off. But then I realize, we should keep it as natural as possible. If she really did just "pass" in her sleep, it would have been while watching Victor and Jack duke it out. Loudly. Plus, this isn't my murder.

This isn't my murder. Did I really just think that?

Stoney approaches Gracie, holding this new pillow with much more respect. He must find the noise from the soap as unnerving as I do because, once again, he hits the pause button.

Reclined and calm, Gracie says, "It still smells like him, you know. Even though it's been months, I can still smell him on it. I can." She closes her eyes again, leans back and relaxes.

"Are you sure?" Stoney asks again.

"Yes." She smiles wearily. "It's time." Then, with a blind nod toward the television, she says, "I'll miss you Victor." With a light cackle, she asks, "Do you think they have my stories in Heaven?"

Stoney smiles, I assume he is as reassured as I am by her attempt to put him at ease. "It's okay," she whispers.

"It's okay. It's okay," he repeats.

He takes her hand in his, the skin so translucent I can almost see the blue of her veins from here. His young, strong hand swallows hers. She squeezes his as best she can, weak, yet firm at the same time. Suddenly Stoney is choked up, forcing back tears. Emotion catches in my throat.

Gracie places both hands serenely on her lap. "Thank you," she murmurs.

We all watch as Stoney gently presses the pillow to her face, gradually adding pressure.

This is how you should die, I think and swallow past the thickness in my throat, *after a long life at the hands of someone who loves you*. It's a wonderful thought, but I am suddenly angry at the unfairness of it.

Time seems to stand still. Stoney balances lightly on the balls of his feet as his extended arms lock. There is a brief convulsion through her body.

After what seems like an eternity, but really only the duration of one more pause cycle, Stoney fumbles for her wrist so frail, so light. Any heart palpitations would resonate and he'd feel them. Shit, I feel so attuned to her, I think I'd feel them from across the room.

He tries again, just to confirm. Balancing the pillow over her face, he uses both hands to lift and check one wrist, then the other. Nothing. That's it. It's over. *It's okay.*

Stoney shivers, suddenly and violently, a gasp chokes his throat and tears emerge. Not my tears, but I feel them, hot and somehow necessary. He exits our view with Frank's pillow.

Returning to the living room, Stoney puts the remote within Gracie's reach, beside the popcorn bag. He looks around. Everything seems normal, well, as normal as when we arrived. He hasn't really touched anything. Except Gracie.

Gracie is resting in the corner of the couch, afghan tucked neatly around her small frame. Her head is tilted back, like she's napping comfortably. A smile still lingers around the corners of her mouth.

Rick, Freddy, and I, the kitchen spectators, approach Stoney, but he dismisses us with a flip of his hand.

Freddy cannot take his eyes off of Gracie's body. She looks like she's sleeping, but still, he's a little green. He keeps swallowing, his Adam's apple lunging up and down. I imagine it's working overtime to hold back the bile that's creeping up from his belly.

I'm pretty sure, I too, am in shock. I cannot believe what Stoney has done. I admire and respect him for it. First, a dad, now, a mercy killer. He wasn't kidding when he said things have changed.

3:53 p.m.

Rick is livid. With red face and puffed cheeks, he reminds me of a Loony Tunes character. I expect smoke to come out curling of his ears any minute. You can tell he is biting back words. At least he has that much sense. I know what's coming; I just spent twenty minutes in a stifling kitchen with him.

Stoney walks over to Gracie, readjusts her hands on her lap. She looks so peaceful, so content. I feel myself getting choked up again. I clear my throat, it's loud and I'm sorry for the interruption.

"Don't forget the pocket money," Rick sneers.

Still standing beside the sofa, Stoney gently folds the afghan back and removes the contents of the housecoat pocket. A rumpled tissue, a partially unwrapped butterscotch disc, and a frayed fabric pocketbook. He replaces the tissue and candy.

In this moment, I imagine we are all reminiscing. Tissues and butterscotch hard candies are so distinctly grandmotherly.

Stoney pockets the coin purse. He doesn't open it or skim through its contents. The amount is not important. He adjusts the blanket again, repositioning her fragile hands, strokes her cheek, then walks toward the kitchen.

He stops, takes one last look around, one last long look at Gracie.

I look, too. I didn't know her, but I hope she's happy. With Frank.

Wiping an escaped tear, Stoney lifts a hand of farewell in her direction. His job here is done. He's made his last delivery.

Stoney turns and walks through the kitchen to the back door. He closes it behind Freddy, the last one out, and replaces the key beneath the pot. We walk solemnly to the car and get in.

Before all four doors are even shut, Rick is venting. "That doesn't count!" he shouts. He's pounding his hands on the dashboard. "It's cheating. Nope, not even—it just doesn't count!" His voice is growing in volume and he's shoving his seat into my knees.

In my most fiercely calm voice, I say, "Shut up." We have exited the alley and are on a residential road again. "This is a quiet neighborhood. You are bringing unwanted attention to us."

With one last slam, he jerks towards the window to sulk.

Stoney drives. We don't know where we're going, none of us, so he's driving aimlessly. I think it's good, though. Therapeutic. Gives us all a chance to let it sink in. Especially Stoney. I'm sure he wishes he had a minute alone to process. I think he'll be okay. I think he *is* okay. But out of respect for Gracie, I wish he had his minute. An opportunity to decompress, process—what did my professor call it? Psychological debriefing. An animated image of Stoney with underpants on his head causes me to laugh out loud.

"Inappropriate. Sorry," I mumble, hoping he didn't hear and think I find Gracie's death funny.

It's nice that the car is cooling down quickly. And it's kind of neat to drive around our 'home' town, seeing places I haven't seen since we were cutting around on dirt bikes. After about ten minutes of random driving, Rick says we need to talk. Stoney responds with, "Where?"

"How about the diner," I reply, shooting Freddy a quizzical look, *you okay to be around food?* it asks. Freddy shrugs and returns to staring blankly out the window.

We pull into Futterman's Diner, *Best Blue Plate in Town!* This place has been family owned for so long, the babies come out smelling like grease. The walk from the car to the restaurant is enough to ruin the chill buzz I had going. I cannot believe how hot it is. Futterman's is cool and comfortable and almost immediately I forget about the weather. We slide into a back booth with ancient red vinyl that's been cracked, then taped, and worn smooth again.

Donna, the waitress, comes over to take our order. Rick practically growls at her. "We need some privacy," he barks. Donna backs away with that 'fuck you' look only seasoned staff can properly convey.

Truth be told, Donna's disdain goes much deeper than her livelihood.

Once again, I tell Rick to shut up. "Quit being an asshole, you're going to make people suspicious."

He glares at me across the table, then shifts his angry face to Stoney, seated to my left. "That did not count," he says tightly under his breath.

"Wait," I say, "let's order something, make it look natural. Four old buddies catching up over some grub at the

111

local diner. Donna's cool, if we tell her to give us some time after the food comes, she will. She's all about not having to check on a customer every five seconds or so, especially us."

"Especially you," Stoney says.

"Yeah, yeah, whatever," I say with a smile.

Rick grumbles, but he snatches a menu off the table and begins perusing.

Freddy'd been holding a menu since we sat down. "I'll have some fries and a 7-Up," he says to no one in particular. He still looks a little peaked and I know he's hoping he can keep that down.

Stoney doesn't bother with a menu. Neither do I. We've come here so often, we practically have it memorized. Not that I need to, I only order one thing.

Rick slaps down his menu and motions for Donna to return. Even though she'd been staring in our direction, she takes her sweet time making her way over to our booth. "Yeah," she says with a 'fuck you' snap of her gum.

"Sorry about that," Rick offers, oozing with charm. He flashes her his rich boy smile, all dazzling white and molars, and I see her relax a bit. They have a history, too, brief as it may be, but that's not what this is. People, especially women, get stupid around pretty people. Add money to the mix and it's easy to see how pretty, rich people rule the world.

Donna's older than we are and still waitressing. What woman wouldn't be interested in committing herself to the likes of Mr. Harris? I guarantee she doesn't give two shits about his college or fraternity statuses. *Stati?* I need a hobby.

"Yeah?" she repeats, but without the accent of snapping gum.

112

Rick responds in a voice so syrupy I am faced with the choice of gagging or smirking. I go with the silent smile. "What's the pie today? I feel like something sweet." He offers her innocent eyes and a dangerous smile.

She's blushing. The bad attitude has melted away from her posture. "We've got apple, lemon meringue, and mixed berry. I'd go with the mixed berry," she adds with a conspiratorial whisper. "It's the freshest.

"Oooh, fresh." His words are engorged with flirtation. "Mixed berry it is," Rick decides. "I'll need a cup of coffee, too." I half expect him to swat her ass as he adds, "Oh, and how about a scoop of vanilla on the side, sweetheart?"

Sweetheart? I just about choke on my spit. It's frightening how quickly he can turn the charm on…and off. You'd think Donna would see right through his manipulations, but like I said, pretty, rich, bad boys make girls stupid.

Donna writes down Rick's order, then nods to Freddy.

"I'll have fries and a 7-Up," he says.

"Sprite okay? Large or small?"

"Small fry." Gulp. "Large Sprite.

"Okay," she writes, turning to Stoney. "What'll it be?"

"You know what I like," Stoney says with a leer-less grin. If he's trying out a Rick move, he's failing, but it gets the job done as she shoots him a look. As far as I know, they don't have a personal history. "Okay, okay," he jokes. "I'll have an open-faced burger, medium-well, pickles on the side. And a Coke."

"You want fries with that?" She's snapping her gum again, but out of habit, not insolence.

113

Stoney glances at the menu splayed on the table. "You know what? I'm mighty hungry. I think I'll have an order of fries and an order of onion rings." He looks up, closing the menu with a slap of sticky laminated pages.

Freddy's and my eyes meet across the table, we mirror raised eyebrows.

Finally, Donna acknowledges me. We dated once upon a million years ago for like a minute. Honestly, I don't even know if you could use the word "dated". She was my first, as in *first*.

She used to babysit for Rick's sister, Michelle. What does that tell you about the Harris' family sensibilities? Hiring a young co-ed to watch over their daughter and oh, by the way, here's our teenage son and all his horny friends. We hooked up one weekend when she was babysitting overnight. I can only imagine that Lupita was on a well-deserved vacation.

Donna was getting paid to play Mommy while Rick's parents were out of town. I guess she thought I was the Daddy. I guess maybe for that weekend I was. They say you never forget your first sexual encounter, but I'm telling you, recollection is directly related to your level of intoxication. I've heard it's usually the girl that gives it up drunk, and I'm not proud of my deflowering circumstances, but hey, whatever. I don't really remember what happened, but I do know there was tequila, a pool, loose swimsuits and scraped knees involved. I think I was just relieved to have it over with. I never really thought about it being anything more than what I barely remembered.

I never really thought about it at all. She did, though. I guess I should have called.

I gather the menus up off the table and hand them to her with a wink. Pressing my luck, I say, "I'll have my usual."

She writes something down, says, "Fine, shit on a shingle it is."

"And a Coke," I add helpfully.

Snatching the menus from me, she turns sharply and stalks away.

"You should have called," Stoney says as Freddy and Rick both nod. Even though it's been seven years, it's like high school all over again. Besides, everybody knows she bedded Rick to get back at me.

"You know she spits in your food, don't you?" Rick says, grinning.

I shrug, "Yeah, we've swapped bodily fluids before, no big deal."

Freddy makes gagging sounds and I can't tell if he's kidding or not.

Then I say, "No, she won't spit in my food, because she still wants me." We all get a good long chuckle out of that.

As soon as Donna is out of earshot, Rick turns in the booth to face us. He's dead serious. Charm on/charm off. "We need to talk."

Stoney sits up, folds his hands on the table in front of him, and says calmly, "Okay."

Rick leans in as close to Stoney as the Formica will allow. "What the fuck, man? That didn't count! We said no women!"

"No. We said 'no purses'." Stoney holds his ground, doesn't flinch, even though I'm pretty sure spittle flew from Rick's mouth and landed mighty close to his own.

"Gracie didn't use a purse. She had a pocketbook, where she kept her money and which she kept in her pocket. Therefore, *pocket money*."

"Fine, whatever. IT DOESN'T COUNT."

The only two other diners sneak a look in our direction and I imagine them swapping stories about those damn punk kids. "Shhh," I say.

Backing down, regaining control, Rick says, "You knew her."

"Yes, and I knew she was ready to go."

"Doesn't count."

"Don't care."

Rick is so frustrated I'm afraid he's going to pop a blood vessel. Who would get credit for that death? Gracie? That's not fair, she can't be a member of our club.

Stoney shrugs, fingers drumming on the tabletop. He is probably the most content I've ever seen him.

Donna brings our drinks and Stoney sucks his Coke halfway down with one sip. "Ah," he sighs and stifles a burp.

Silence but for the sound of shifting ice in the cups.

Continued silence, long and awkward, even the ice is quiet.

"How much did you..." Rick musters.

He is interrupted by Donna with our food and another drink for Stoney.

Passing out our orders, she serves mine last, sliding the dish in front of me with a flip of her wrist which makes the plate bounce on the table with a thump and a splatter of brown.

"Thanks, Donna," I say, acknowledging the savory droplets on my shirt. "I'll be saving those for later." I make lip-smacking sounds even as I wipe them with a napkin.

It's not shit on a shingle or crap from a can or cheez whiz surprise. It's the house special, meatloaf, and it's amazing. Yes, meatloaf. Seasoned to perfection, cut thick with bits of onion, oh, good stuff. I shudder when I see someone glop ketchup on it. That seems so…disrespectful. Futterman's meatloaf is better than any I've ever had, anywhere.

I'm not really hungry, having eaten that pizza just a few short/long hours ago, but I can't come in here and not order the special. Besides, it's the closest I've come to a home cooked meal in a really long time. I eye it with anticipation, my taste buds salivating. Meatloaf, good old-fashioned comfort food. I could use some comfort about now.

Once served, Stoney tells Donna thanks and we'll let her know if we need anything else. She gets the hint and wanders off to check on her other customers. We've come at a slow time, after the lunch crowd but before the blue hair happy hour.

We focus on our food for a few minutes. Freddy picks gingerly at his fries, no ketchup, just potatoes. Bite, chew, swallow. Slowly he comes to the understanding that they will stay down. He relaxes a bit and begins to enjoy.

Rick also seems to be picking at his fare. I don't think he really wanted pie, that was all for Donna's sake. Plus, he's still in a dick mood. He cradles his coffee cup and glares balefully over the rim at Stoney.

Stoney is oblivious. He is digging in, cutting, chomping, dipping, smacking, chewing, practically shoveling. He, too,

117

ate his fill of pizza a short time ago, but I guess it was literally a lifetime for him. There's a smudge of ketchup on his upper lip, which he either doesn't notice or is keeping as a tribute to his enjoyment of this meal. He keeps looking at each of us as he attacks his food. He is almost beaming. I'm torn between relief and concern.

Rick looks down at his dessert plate. He has dissected it with his fork, but not actually eaten any. Between stabs and tosses of his pie, he asks, "So how much did you get? You know," he scoffs, "in pocket money?"

Stoney raises his brows, still chewing. He replaces a freshly ketchupped onion ring on his plate and digs into his pocket. He removes the weathered coin purse, unzips it, and dumps the contents on the table between my plate and his.

There is a rolled stack of bills and some change. Mostly pennies. A lot of pennies. I don't know why, but that sticks with me. Old people value pennies. *What do we value?*

Stoney carefully fingers the bills, counting and fanning the curling paper for all to see. "Thirty-six dollars," he says. He sighs, shuffling the bills back into a single pile before folding them gently. He tucks the stack in his pocket. Then he slides the change off the table and lets it drop into the waiting pouch. He zips it up and shoves it in another pocket. Then he resumes eating, although slower and without eye contact.

Rick cough-laughs loudly. "Thirty-six dollars!" He forces a chuckle, the sound rough and grating to my ears. "That'll what? Cover your lunch?" He slaps the table, making his fork dance off the plate with a berry spray. "You are such a loser. And I mean that in every sense of the word. Loo-oo-zer." He's just getting going. "Why would you cheat, break our own rules, for a lousy thirty-six bucks?" He whistles through his teeth, shoves his pie plate forward, clinking it into Stoney's, puts his elbows on the table and says, "Dumbass."

Finally, Stoney wipes his face, tosses the used napkin on his empty platter and sits back. "Okay," he looks from Freddy to Rick and back again. "Who's next?"

Freddy and Rick look at each other. They are not exchanging glances as much as battling eyeballs.

"Not me," says Rick. "I told you, I'm working on a plan."

Awkward silence ensues as Freddy seems to shrink into the booth.

"Hey, Fred," I offer, "if you want to bail on this, we understand."

"What the—" Rick begins, but I silence him with a glare.

"It's crazy, really. Totally mental what we're doing, what we started. You don't have to play along. Stop now, before it's too late to take anything back." Desperate as I am for my pleas to be heard, for sense to trump absurdity, I'm trying to keep it casual for Freddy's sake.

"No, I'm good," Freddy says, sitting up a little straighter. "Let's go." It's obvious he has no plan. He looks unsure and his pallor has returned, but I know there's no backing down in front of Rick.

Remembering his sickly tinge following the very sedate and compassionate passing of Gracie, I give it one more shot. "C'mon, Freddy, it's cool." I pause, trying to figure out how to spin this. "Hey," I say with overt enthusiasm, "I bet we're not going to believe what happened to you..."

Freddy smiles weakly. "Thanks, but no." He meets Rick's accusatory stare. "I need to do this."

4:45 p.m.

"Well, come on!" presses Rick. "What are we doing? You're up, dude. What's the plan?" Bouncing in the booth, he's reinvigorated. I guess he's forgotten Stoney's transgression. The game is on and Rick is in it to win it.

My half-eaten meatloaf burbles heavily in my gut.

"I gotta sieve," I say, motioning Stoney to scoot over and let me out.

"Huh?" asks Freddy.

"Pee, man. I hafta take a leak."

"Oh," he says, pushing on Rick's shoulder. "Me, too."

"Whoa," I say.

"Dude," Stoney explains, "we're guys."

"One at a time," I add. I slide off the vinyl bench and head toward the rest room in the back. I wonder if there's a window in there I could escape through. My belly is full, my head is fuller. We're halfway through a murder club initiation and a little bit, it's freaking me out. I pick a stall as opposed to the urinal, even though I'm still standing. Living in the dorms ruined me for public urination. I read the graffiti as I take care of business and wonder if I had a pen would I add, "For a good time call Donna"? But then I realize that with or without a pen, I don't know her number.

Freddy is waiting by the table for his turn like it's a relay race. I fist bump him on my way past. "All yours."

121

Rick waves for Donna, drumming on the table. Switch on. Or maybe it's the caffeine from his coffee kicking in. A guy can dream, right?

Donna comes over, places the check between us, pauses slightly not knowing if she should stay or come back.

"Hey, Donna, do you have to-go cups?" Stoney asks from my seat, sucking the last remnants of his Coke through the straw with a loud gurgle.

"Uh, sure," she says. "Anybody else?"

See, she can't stay mad at me. We all shake our heads, no. I don't know about these guys, but I am at capacity. And waning. I need a nap. Thoughts of escape again fill my head and I realize I never checked for a bathroom window. If there is one, I wonder if Freddy is halfway through it.

"Be right back," Donna says.

Rick grins. "Thanks, doll. C'mon on guys, pony up," he says as Freddy returns.

The bill is passed around. Everybody digs out their cash. I cover my part and toss in an extra three bucks towards tip. It's easy, knowing I have found money in my other pocket.

Freddy is counting out singles. I know he's hoping we're each taking responsibility for our own tab and not splitting the bill four ways. He only had a small fry and large Sprite, and besides, he's got no money.

Stoney reaches into his pants for his cash, pulls out a wad and stops suddenly. He carefully extracts Gracie's bills from the rest and shoves it in the pocket with the coin purse. He flicks through his own money and slaps some on the pile. I assume he's added tip, too, but I don't check. My mother was a waitress for many years; I'm sensitive to tipping. It's damn hard work. If I can't tip well, I don't eat out. I don't usually eat out.

Rick scoops up our pile, fingering the crumpled bills like they're foreign material to him. Scoffing, he lets the dollars fall to the table top. "Just kidding, boys." He pulls a money clip from one of his shorts' pockets, and a tiny plastic packet flies out onto the worn carpet.

Each one of us reacts. Stoney clucks in disgust, Freddy looks away, and Rick snatches it in the time it takes me to ask him what the fuck is that.

Ignoring me, he peels two fifties from his fat clip and slaps them down. He slides them in Donna's direction as she hands Stoney a white Styrofoam cup with lid and straw.

"Keep the change, doll." Rick winks at her and stands.

Donna practically swoons. I swear I can see her knees weaken, as she picks up the cash and slips it, not into her apron pocket, no, but into her blouse. I catch a glimpse of pink bra as she flashes Rick a quick peek.

In response, Rick presses down the front of his cargo shorts and adjusts accordingly.

I'm tempted to interrupt this floor show with a grab of my own dick, but of course, I don't.

Instead I slink out of the booth with Freddy following. He scrapes together the leftover cash with no air of guilt or embarrassment. He leads our pack to the door. There's pep in his step. He's got a plan. He holds the door for us to file through, back out into the heat and humidity. Grabbing Stoney by the arm as he passes, Freddy asks, "Can I drive your car?"

To which I think, *I don't know, can you?*

"Uh, sure, I guess." Stoney is a little apprehensive, but tosses the keys to Freddy then walks around to the front passenger side, cutting Rick off cleanly.

"Hey!" Rick shouts.

"Hey," Stoney replies. "My car, my shotgun."

4:52 p.m.

Freddy behind the wheel of a car is a scary thing. He doesn't have a lot of experience. Thankfully, he seems to have a destination, so he drives with focus. After the mirror and seat adjustments, he checks all his points, put the car in reverse and backs out. He won't tell us where we're going, despite constant badgering from Rick.

"Shut up," Stoney whispers to Rick. "You're distracting him." I know Stoney is curious as to our destination, too, but he keeps quiet. Out of respect for Freddy or concern for his car? Doesn't matter.

I'm still pissed about the drugs. "So, hey, Rick, what's up with the blow?"

No response.

I knock my knee into his. "Yo, I'm talking to you."

"Shhh," he says, motioning towards Freddy. "Driving."

What the fuck. He knows how I feel about hard drugs. About coke specifically. *He knows.* I press my forehead to the window, close my eyes, and talk myself through the anger.

I smoke pot. It's not a confession; it's just, well, to be honest, I consider it a psych major's rite of passage. I've never done cocaine or crack or heroin or any of that shit. Bad shit. Scary shit.

The tears come without warning, slamming my ducts and spilling over my cheeks. I turn my face further away, rolling my head against the glass almost till my opposite ear touches. I squeeze my lids together, pressing until I see stars bloom in the blackness. I sing the song in my head until the urge passes. Ironically, our song placates me.

Adjusting my body upright against the seat, I lay my arm over my face as my head presses the headrest. "Damn, I'm tired," I say, yawning to cover the hitch in my voice.

I hate this fuckin' day.

5:02 p.m.

When I've collected myself emotionally, I stare through burning eyes out the window and wonder where we're going. Day like this, could be anywhere.

Freddy heads out of town, past the industrial park with its huge buildings and sprawling factories, too many of which are abandoned. Barren and broken, a sad remembrance of a better time in our economy, reflecting the financial status of a lot of our city's families. A true metaphor for a lot of our lives. We drive past the airport, past farms and fields, and lots and lots of nothingness. Oh, and cows.

Rick is getting really impatient. "Where are we going? What's your plan? This is stupid. You probably don't even have a plan. Just wasting our time. My time. And Stoney's gas." He shoves the back of the driver's headrest.

Once again, I have to wonder if Rick is afraid we're going to take him out. Like this whole day, this whole murder club, er, gang, is an elaborate ruse to get him out alone and off him. What would we possibly have to gain by killing our high school friend? Or better yet, why is he so fucking paranoid?

The obvious train comes to a slow halt at my brain station. Nevermind, stupid question. Fuckin' coke. I don't

127

know how I missed it before, but now that I know, I can't unnotice the signs.

I'm tempted to shush Rick and his chatter but Freddy says, "We're almost there," as he turns into the forest preserve. A plane passes over us, forming a shadow cross on the sprouted fields.

"What the hell?" Rick says irritably. "You gonna kill a critter?" Smirking, he says, "I told Stoney and I'm telling you, *it doesn't count.*" On a roll, "Let me clarify, Freddy, wabbits don't have wawwwets." He busts out laughing. Then, realizing the error of his comment, he adds, "Or pockets."

"Leave the impressions to Fr—" Stoney begins.

"Shush." This from Freddy. Sternly.

Stunned silence from the three of us.

Freddy is driving very slowly, rounding curves and climbing hills, followed by more curves and valleys. It is a beautiful park. There's a river and a quarry buried in these wooded acres. We used to come here for field trips when we were kids. I'm pretty sure I still have the first real fossil I ever found in this quarry. It's a bivalve perfectly outlined in limestone. I smile at the memory. Sure, that I remember, but I couldn't call Donna. Go figure.

We wander at a time-killing park pace past the cabin, still closed for the season, coasting over the bridge that spans the Marsasauga River, wide and deep at this juncture—a popular place for summer boating, and into parts of the park where I have never ventured.

Rick is shifting around in the back seat. Completely discontent. "Listen you dumb-fuck," he starts when suddenly Freddy punches the gas pedal. The car surges forward, pressing us back against the padded seat as he accelerates.

The car shudders and there's a thud, followed by a thunk, and Freddy brakes hard. Rick and I are slammed into the seats in front of us.

It takes a minute to regroup. Freddy is laughing maniacally. He puts the car in park but leaves it running as he unclasps his belt and jumps out. He is giggling like a school girl at a Marky Mark concert. He covers his mouth to try to keep it in as he runs around to the front of the car. In his hurry, he trips over a fat rock on the side of the road and goes flying across the gravel road. He jumps ups, not missing a beat, not noticing the abraded knees and palms that are sprouting beads of blood. When he sees his victim, he begins jumping up and down and clapping.

Recovered from the momentum assault, Rick and I look at each other before slowly getting out.

Stoney, being shotgun, is there first. "Shit, Freddy!" he yelps, dropping to his knees. "What'd you do?"

Having taken the long way around, Rick comes up on Stoney's side and stops short, "Well, fuck me."

Even though I know what is causing the commotion, I'm still stunned by the crumpled hiker lying twisted a few feet from Stoney's bumper.

It's a guy, about our age, maybe a little older. He is bent and broken and bleeding. But just a little blood, I notice. A trickle from his mouth and gashes across the sides of his upper calves. His legs are splayed at unnatural angles, as is his neck.

I swallow hard, and close my eyes for a moment. Exhaling slowly, I open them and assess.

The dead guy is wearing lightweight break-away hiking pants that have broken away in all the wrong places. The rips reveal split skin, blood oozing around white bone. I cringe at how bad that must hurt then chastise myself for such stupidity.

Freddy drops down on all fours and begins ransacking the guy's pockets. His hands are shaking like a kid on Christmas searching for the best present. There are multiple pants' pockets and a vest with even more options. Freddy is diligently going through them.

Stoney places a restraining hand against Freddy's shoulder, pushing him back. "Maybe we should check for a pulse first."

"Maybe we should get the fuck out of here!" Rick screams, looking around frantically.

Rick's breath is coming fast and shallow and I smile, on the inside. Mr. In Control, President of the Murder Club. Yeah, right.

When the hiker groans and his eyes flutter, I imagine Rick jumps out of his skin, but it is Freddy who reacts the fastest by grabbing that tripping boulder and bashing the guy in the head. Once, twice, hard, before Stoney can stop him.

But why stop him? I wonder. *Isn't this the point?* The point of the whole fucked up day.

Now there is a lot of blood. The hiker's face is crushed, his eyeballs squishing through fractured sockets, red teeth bared and broken behind flaps that used to form lips. I turn away before I risk seeing brain matter.

Stoney feels for a pulse while I check for damage to his car. I know he has to be worried about that, too, but Stoney is too much of a humanitarian to make that his first priority. I am much too squeamish to look anywhere else.

I run my hand across the hood, feeling the indentation the hiker's head made when it bounced off. I bend to check the front end. I see a minor dent in the bumper that might predate this collision and several cracks in the grill. Some old, some new. Some now. Upon closer inspection, I can see bits of fabric and scrapes of bloody flesh stuck in the strata of bug guts. Fuck.

"Nope. Shit," Stoney says, placing the wrist back on the ground. "No pulse here."

I can see his wheels turning as he considers checking the neck pulse, but that's too close to the damage, to the streaming blood and battered flesh, so he passes. I don't think it matters.

Freddy resumes his pillaging. There are a lot of pockets.

"Granola bar…compass…bug spray…a ha, paper! Shit, maps."

Freddy's frustration is mounting as he digs through pockets, pulling out and shoving back in.

Rick looks on with simmering contempt. I can just imagine what he is thinking, *How much cash can road kill carry?* I'm sure he's assuming his prize is guaranteed. *Good, maybe we can call it a day and go ho—*.

My thoughts are interrupted by Freddy squealing with glee. There is a zippered bag in the lining of the vest, hidden to most but not to thorough Freddy. Inside the pouch he finds a photo ID, Doug Stanford from Beaverton, Oregon, and several crisp new bills. Crisp, new *hundred* dollar bills. Four to be exact.

As Freddy is replacing the ID card, he notices a penny in the corner of the pouch. A penny. A lucky fucking penny. He shakes it into the palm of his hand, pockets it, then calmly zips the container back up and replaces it. He snaps up the vest and adjusts the pants' pockets.

As he stands up, the manic returns. Fanning the bills out for everyone to see, he jumps around. "What a wanker," he cries out. "Hiking with one, two, three, *four* hundred dollar bills!"

In my head, I hear the Count from Sesame Street barking his dark laugh.

Freddy repeats, "Four hundred!" He waves the fan playfully in each of our faces.

Rick smacks his hand. "Yeah? What now? Can't leave him here."

"I know," says Freddy, still dancing. Folding the bills with care, he sticks the money in his pants, then pauses with his hands on his hips, surveying the situation. Inhaling a deep breath, he grabs one of the guy's arms. "Little help?"

Stoney dutifully lifts the other arm and they begin dragging the body across the road, down the ravine and into the woods.

Smoothing out the drag marks, I catch up and take the guy's booted feet in my hands.

Freddy seems uncharacteristically familiar with these woods as he leads us through some low brush and then up an overgrown path. At the top of this hill is a cliff. Not the quarry I mentioned, just a large dip in the forest terrain. It's thick with trees and jutting limestone.

"Untie his shoe," Freddy directs me. I drop one leg and begin futzing with the lace of the other. It's tricky, there are eyelets and hooks. These are fancy hiking boots. Expensive. Complicating matters further are the brambles and burrs that glue the laces to each other.

"Okay," I say.

"Grab him good and swing," Freddy tells us, "on three."

Stoney and I look at each other with dark understanding.

"Three," says Freddy, and we release.

Doug, I hardly knew ye.

The body is airborne for about six feet, then it drops. It tumbles for five yards, skipping over rocks, bouncing around trees, and plowing through bushes. His shoe flies off into the thicket.

Swiping his hands back and forth against each other, signifying a job well done, Freddy says, "Thanks, guys," and heads back to the car. I am amazed at his poise. I mean, this is Freddy for fuck's sake.

When he sees the bloody rock, the boulder he bashed the guy's head in with, he turns and pukes into the ravine. He falls to his knees, the retching deep; it doesn't take long for the small fry and large soda to make a reappearance.

"Come on, man," Stoney says, helping Freddy to his feet. He guides him back to the car and settles him in the back seat.

With the toe of my tennis shoe, I roll the boulder across to the shoulder and nudge it into the flood gutter, thankful that it lands murder side down. It hasn't been a terribly wet spring, but there's enough of a flow to hopefully rinse the rock. "Hey," I call to Stoney, my stomach clenching as I nod toward the blood spatters absorbing into the dusty road. Blood mud.

"Shit," he says. Reaching into the car, he gets his to-go cup. He removes the lid and hands it to me. I drip and kick until there's no way anyone could recognize what caused this mess. In today's sun, with this heat, it will be dry before we're out of the park.

And, there's the urban legend about Coke killing DNA working for us, too.

5:30 p.m.

The car is still in the road, still running, three of the four doors are still open. Rick is in the front passenger seat, arms crossed, glaring.

Stoney slams Freddy's door as we get in, close our doors, and sit there, idling. Freddy is hunched over in the back seat, mumbling to himself. His arms are crossed tightly and I can see he's retrieved the cash from his pocket and holds it in a death grip. *Death grip*, I'm so clever.

Stoney adjusts the seat so his knees can breathe, and the mirrors so he can see, then puts the car in gear and accelerates slowly, leaving the mess and the death behind. It takes another twenty minutes and two and a half miles to exit the preserve. Stoney heads back toward town.

"You okay?" I ask Freddy, patting his shoulder. *I cannot fucking believe this just happened.*

He shrugs. "Yeah," he says.

Naw, I think.

Sitting up, a tear sneaks out of one eye. "It's just weird, you know?" Freddy says. "I just…I never—" He swipes his eye with the edge of a fist.

"I know," I say. We both turn to look out our respective windows.

"Where to?" Stoney asks a still sullen Rick.

135

In response, Rick grumbles. His arms are crossed, then uncrossed. He's tugging against the seatbelt, shuffling his feet.

"Eh? Excuse me?" Stoney asks. "Home, James? Call it a day?"

Yes.

"No!" Rick punches the dashboard, hard.

"We don't have to do this, you know. There's nothing to prove," I say. I clear my throat, buying some time before I launch into what I should've said from the beginning. I look across the back seat at Freddy who is still clutching those bills. It's too late for him. I say it anyway. "What if I told you I found that wallet? Yeah, I did. Found it in the parking lot when I stopped to get detergent this morning."

"Bullshit," Rick snarls. "Don't even bother."

I force a laugh and it comes out like a seal bark. "Really, you are not going to believe what happened to me…"

I'm staring at Freddy when he looks up at me with big round eyes, his dark eyebrows arcing high.

"Yep," I say. "Just a story."

Rick starts to swear at me again, on the verge of a litany of colorful name-calling when Stoney interrupts. "We know what today is," he says quietly. That shuts Rick up. And jerks me to attention. Suddenly rigid and angry, I ask what he means. He tells me. Tells me what I already know, what I could never forget. What I didn't think they knew. What I'd gone years not telling.

"We're sorry," he says. "About Allie."

Hearing her name is like a punch to my heart. I gasp, the air forced out with the emotional blow.

"Told ya' I ran into your mom," Rick says, like that explains this psyche hijack.

I catch Stoney's gaze in the rear view mirror. "How come you never told us you had a sister?"

I shrug and look away. I guess because I *had* a sister, as in, I don't anymore. Allie was my sister, my half-sister. We have the same mom, but different dads.

I close my eyes, steeling back the onslaught of stinging tears once again. What did my mom tell him? How much do they know?

My mind is filled with Allie, our last moments together. They play out in vivid Technicolor and slow motion. My baby sister and I beneath the neighbor's porch, not a fun sibling adventure, no, but hiding from the emotional pyrotechnics on our front lawn.

In the back seat of Stoney's car, but tossed back in time, I tremble as I glance over Allie's shoulder. Through ten years and the slatted wall that conceals us, I see her father knocking our mother around. The neighbor's porch beneath which we hide is not far enough away to drown out the screams, the yells, the drunken angry accusations, but it was where we could get in the time we had.

I try to distract her, to comfort her, by singing. "*Daisy, Daisy, give me your answer do…*" The same song that brought me peace just a few short miles ago echoes through my head, "*I'm half crazy, all for the love of you…*"

Here, like there, my peripheral vision is not as vivid as my memory. I can't really see, but I see. We had been there before. We would be there again, or so I thought. Even after all this time, I still wonder why no one called the police. Why no one intervened on the battered woman's behalf. On

137

behalf of her four year old daughter a single property line away, or even for the benefit of her twelve year old son cowering beneath a porch with the dirt and trash and scat of previous residents. I remember seeing their peering faces beside pulled curtains. I knew they were judging and was at a loss at to why their behavior—their inaction—was any better, or worse, than the actions they were judging. They might as well have been busting their own knuckles on her jaw. My teeth clench at the recollection and the tears burn rivulets down my cheeks.

I had talked myself down then, for Allie, and, all of these years later, I find I have to do it again, for me.

I can't break from the scene playing out in my brain. There's a term for this, you know. Memory hoarding. The inability to escape the minutia of an experience.

As if it were happening in real time, I hear the sound of crashing plaster. A booted foot topples the base of a plant stand and Allie flinches. Her blue eyes go wide and her lower lip quivers.

Stay with me, my gaze commands. I'm reaching out with my right hand and rubbing the space above her inner wrist—in this case, my thigh where the wire abrasion is, but I swear, I can feel her cool, tender arm. Then I stroke her ear, my thumb touching softly just below the upper fold. I'd researched this, ways to distract, soothe. Looked it up in the school library. Even back then I had an interest in the study of psychology. I knew I couldn't get her away, but maybe I could take her mind off the episode at her back.

The song continues through my brain, the soundtrack to this nightmare. "*It won't be a fancy marriage—*" I pause here, as I did then. I'd give her a nod of my head and a slight

138

smile. This was her favorite line because it was so silly. "We can't get married," she liked to tell me, "we're already 'elated!"

A sob escapes but I can't stop mid-memory. Part of me is so angry at them for setting me on this path, part of me relieved.

I'd been singing that song to her since we first met, long before she would even consciously remember. We'd just come from dinner at Shakey's Pizza. Do you remember? That place with the player piano and old timey tunes? We used to go there for family nights once in a while. On good days.

When my mom asked if I'd like to talk to the baby, I gaped at her emerging belly, then looked at her like she was crazy. She'd laughed and said that the doctor mentioned studies showing that newborns react positively to familiar voices. I didn't know what to say, so I started singing the old timey song that was stuck in my head. It became "our" song.

My eyes are squinched together in 1992, but in 1982, I dare to peek past Allie's fair hair to check on the lawn activity. I try not to flinch in kind as I see him throw a much younger version of our mother to the ground again. Then, as now, I tell that mother to stop trying to calm him down. Stop trying to not make him angry. It's not working. *Stop, stop, stop.*

Allie didn't respond with her childish bubbly, "already 'elated", so I'd continued, thinking this melee would have to be over soon. "*I can't afford a carriage…*"

I had often considered intervening myself, especially after that growth spurt that shot me up past him. My dad was a big guy, tall and broad. I know this from stories and old photographs, not because I'd ever met him. At least he had the decency to leave my mom and me. Allie's dad should have been so considerate. He was a smidge shorter than mom. He'd never hurt me or Allie. Yet. But he was a mean drunk. Sober, he could charm honey from a hive. Maybe that's how people justified their lack of intervention. *He's such a nice guy, it must be her fault.* It wasn't.

I didn't want Allie to only associate the song with terror, so I sang it to her frequently. When I walked her to school, pushed her on the swings, or rode with her on my bike— those were some of her favorite things. Sometimes I changed up the words just to see if she was paying attention. *Allie, Allie, give me some Kool-Aid, too, I'm so thirsty for your grape bug juice.* I wanted this song to remind her of me, of love and security and silliness.

The song reminds me of everything; the good, the bad, the worst.

Mrs. Harvey, our neighbor, would have let us in if she was home. After Mr. Harvey had a heart attack and died, Mrs. Harvey didn't spend much time there anymore. She visited her grown children and traveled. Nothing to be home for. Unless you're a fan of physical fireworks on the adjoining property.

There was a slat of lattice board on the far side of the porch that was rotted loose. We discovered it a few months earlier when our cat crawled through and couldn't find a way back out. Stupid cat yowled for hours till we figured out where he was and how to get to him. I threw a blanket under there once, thinking it'd be nice to have next time, but by then, it was gone. Probably dragged off by a possum or 'coon. An animal smarter than our cat, Bootsy.

The tirade that day seemed different than usual. How sick is it that I can use the word, "usual"? I swallow thickly, my throat dry. I know I can't escape this memory, if only I could fast forward.

Then it was quiet. Allie had turned to look over her shoulder before I could stop her. He was walking toward us, stomping across the Harvey's yard. He raised the back of his hand to his face and looked at the damage, yanking at a flap of skin. I'd pulled her to me and scooted backwards. It was not a large space, but this put us closer to the broken board should an emergency retreat be required.

Through the years, I can hear my mother crying out, her howls echoing from her station on the lawn. She screamed *Stop!* And *Don't!* and *No!*, but he kept walking. I assumed I was his target, always a smart-ass and dumbshit and forever a bastard. A little fuckin' bastard. Moments like this, I couldn't do or say anything that wouldn't piss him off further.

I dragged Allie all the way to the limestone back of the underporch, close to the house. She squeaked at the proximity of the cobwebs and filth, but let me leave her there.

I popped out the side and replaced the board before walking around the front of the house. I didn't know what to say to him, so I focused on my hands, dangling at my sides, totally non-threatening.

"Where is she?" he growled at me and I thought he meant mom. I paused in confusion and that triggered something in him. He staggered forward, already pulling his arm back. I ducked his punch, turned and back-stepped toward our house, away from where Allie was hiding. *Close your eyes*, I begged her, *close your eyes and your ears and give me your answer do...*

"Where is she, you little shit?" He set his feet and swiveled from left to right, scanning.

"Allie?" This time it was I who squeaked.

He lunged, connecting a fist with the side of my head. "Yes, you son of a bitch. Where's Allie? I'm taking my daughter..." He continued but it was muffled and I couldn't understand his words. "Bitch," and "fucking whore," and "save my baby," leaked through. Then—oh my god, he was crying! How to deal with that? The man who just smacked me with my mother's blood on his hands was crying and blubbering about saving his baby, my sister, Allie.

"No," I blurted.

"Allie," he shouted. "Allie!" His nose was bubbling and his stubbled cheeks glistened.

This is where my breath hitches and I try to will myself to the backseat of Stoney's car. I need to be here, to be present, far from what's coming back then.

In my memory, I catch movement out of the corner of my eye as the lattice board falls. "Allie, no," I call. "Stay there!" I remember running to the porch. He was between me and my destination and took this opportunity to put out a steel-toed boot, causing me to go flying. I landed face first, my body following with a thud and snap. "Allie, no," I cried, my voice high. My nose was bleeding, in 1992, I wipe it absently, in 1982, it's flowing into my mouth and mingling with the dirt and grass I ate upon landing.

He doesn't even move, just lets his frightened little daughter stumble towards him. Her cheeks are shiny, her eyes wider than I've ever seen them. Where was my mother?

Why wasn't she helping? I struggled to my knees, my left ankle dragging awkwardly. My foot flopped and I couldn't gain any purchase. Pain shot through my body, but all I could think about was Allie.

He scooped her up, hugging her tight. He pressed his wet face into the blonde hair at the crook of her neck, blubbering about love and getting the hell outta here.

I looked past him to where my mother was standing. Her face was puffy with alternating shades of red and darkness. She cradled an arm. She seemed uncharacteristically calm. Maybe she thought this was the end of today's episode of *The Facts of Strife*, and that we'd resume our regularly scheduled programming.

He had other plans. Shifting Allie to his hip, he fumbled in his pocket for the car keys. This action uprooted my mother who flung herself at him as he passed to the driveway. "Back off, bitch," he'd mumbled.

Allie must've been too scared to scream, she clutched at her father with pinched hands. My mother was tearing at him, pleading, trying to break his grasp on their daughter.

Suddenly I was calling, "*Daisy, Daisy!*" I tried to drag myself behind him but couldn't catch up. Then, as in this moment, I can't help. I am useless, inferior. A smart-ass and a dumbshit and forever a bastard.

With a flip of his arm, he backhanded my mother, the keys in his hand slicing her cheek. To this day, she bears a sliver of scar, a daily reminder. He whipped open the car door and shoved Allie inside. She stared through the window as he slammed her in, cutting off the sound of her sobs. Her chest was heaving and her nostrils flared. I saw her mouth, "Give me your answer do—" and then she was jerked forward, the side of her head bouncing off the window, as he gunned the Granada in reverse. Into the path of a floral delivery truck.

I'm screaming. I feel hands grip me, holding my arm, patting my back, but there is no solace to be had. I've come this far, I must see the memory through. It's the curse of the damaged.

The sound of my keening that day was drowned out by the car horn, engaged by the face of my stepfather. I fell to all fours, the smashed metal and glass shards and wisps of blonde hair the last thing I saw before blacking out.

It had been Ginny Carson's birthday. Ginny lived three houses down from us. Her grandparents had sent her a lovely bouquet with balloons and a card. *Happy 16th Birthday, Ginny! Watch out Other Drivers! Love Grandma and Grandpa Carson* the card had read. I know because it turned up in the gutter a few days later. The ink was blurred and the paper worn, but I could read it and a little bit I hated Ginny and her grandparents and her fucking sixteenth birthday. I still have the card in my wallet.

That was how my suburban family of four became once again a nomadic pair of lost and lonely souls. And also the catalyst for my mother's drug use and eventual abuse. When there is death, there is often denial.

The dazed driver had been wearing his lap belt. His spleen burst. He was in agony but still walked away. I remember a bit, but mostly it's like the edge of a dream upon waking. You can almost grasp it, but not quite. I wish the rest of that day were as hazy.

Sometimes I catch myself singing that song. I laugh and cry at the same time wondering if I'll ever be 'elated again.

5:40 p.m.

"You okay?" Freddy has his hand firmly on my shoulder, but it's Stoney whose voice cuts through the fog. "Sorry, man, didn't mean to send you there."

The car has come to a stop. I look out the window as the others look at me. I feel their eyes, but their gazes are comforting, not judgmental. Even Rick seems to have calmed down. Sympathetic, I suppose, since he could never be empathetic.

We are in the heart of campus, at Mueller Hall, but everybody calls it the "castle building". It's where the university first began and spread out from here. The oldest structure still standing in this town, they just spent millions of dollars and nearly a decade to bring it up to code. This is the first time I've seen it without some sort of scaffolding and construction tape cordoning off one section or another. It boasts turrets and elaborate supports and there are these cool pathways between the corner towers. It even has a mock moat created by stones, plants, and flowers. It's a pretty impressive building.

Suddenly, I need to get out. Out of this space—the one in my head, the back seat of this cramped car, this town, this day. But I will settle for out of the car.

I race from the curb to the nearest side of the castle, the tower by the west entrance. I'm taller and broader than the last time I scaled this building, but my fingers find niches in the stonework as my feet discover accommodating ledges.

I hear the car doors slam, four of them since I'd left mine open, and the shuffle of tennis shoes along the grass then over the sidewalk. A huffing Stoney joins me on the left and an eager Freddy on my right. We're laughing, the three of us, as we inch along the grouted fissures in the façade.

Stoney is lanky and light-fingered, his digits finding placement as if reading the building's instruction in braille. Freddy is nimble and enthusiastic. His laughter is contagious and a bit simian.

Glancing over my shoulder, I see Rick standing on the walkway. His arms are crossed, his head tilted at a "no way" angle. His sunglasses slip to the tip of his nose and he slides them up again before tucking his hand back in the crook of his elbow.

We round one wall and creep into the shade of the corner tower. The break in direct sunlight is a welcome relief. I'm dripping with sweat, wanting desperately to wipe it from my eyes but unable to risk my grip. Freddy is already up and over the edge of the stone sill. He pauses a minute to point and mock me and Stoney, the slow oversized Mueller monkeys.

There was a time when we could keep up, although no time ever existed where we could pass him. I remember scaling 'round these walls for hours, slip off, go back to the beginning and start over. We did this all through junior high and high school, challenging each other to more and more difficult paths. Until that fateful evening in late June when an inebriated Rick slid down the side of the covered parapet and broke his jaw on a jutting barbican. That's actually how I learned those terms, the ambulance tech told us.

When Stoney and I catch up to Freddy on the roof of the new non-castled addition, Rick is already there.

"Fire escape," he says, nodding to the recently painted metal rail.

"Cheater," I gasp, flapping my damp t-shirt against my sweaty chest.

Rick's teeth clench even as Stoney, Freddy and I reach up to touch our rotating jaws. There's a communal grunt of acknowledgement and I say, "Jinx, you all owe me a Coke." Man, I could use an icy Coke right now.

"I can still feel where the wires went in," Rick says, rubbing each side of his jawline, up by his ears.

"Mmm-mff-mm," Freddy mumbles as if his mouth is wired shut.

"Mmm-mff-mm this," Rick responds, flipping him the bird.

"That was so weird," Stoney says. "A whole month of liquids."

"Month? Shit, it was six weeks!"

"By the end, you were putting anything in the blender," I say.

Rick chuckles. "Yeah, chicken noodle soup, pot pies, Spaghettios, Twinkies…"

Stoney, Freddy, and I grimace in unison.

"Mmm, a mashed potato and gravy shake," Rick says, licking his lips.

I plop down against the angle of the roof, next to a sprawled Freddy. I feel good; better than I have all day. Better than I have in a long time. The emotion, the angst, the anger—it's all left me through my flushed pores. Now that we've settled down, I realize I reek.

5:58 p.m.

I lift an arm and stick my nose in the vicinity of my pit, which is totally unnecessary. "Whew, boy. Dang, I stink."

"Man, you arrived stinkin'," Stoney says.

And I imagine that's true since I'm wearing yesterday's clothes. I shrug, flapping my shirt for a breeze once again. "No clean laundry," I say. "Told you that."

I hear the trusty lighter spark to life and glance at Rick. He's sitting on the grated floor of the fire escape, leaning against the metal railing, and lighting a chub. I inhale deeply, the wisps of his smoke enticing me. "Mmm-mff-mm," I say slowly, "having your jaw wired shut didn't slow down the doobage intake."

"Then or ever." The words come out in a gasp, accompanied by a stream of pale white.

He passes it to me and I gladly partake. Finally, my vices are working for me. I hit it two or three times, my lungs expanded to superhuman size, before I offer it to Freddy. He accepts it, passes it to Stoney, who takes it, passes it back to Rick.

"No problem, mon," Rick laughs, "more for us." He inhales deeply, holds it, then sputters, "Speaking of boobs," he says.

That certainly gets our attention.

149

"Remember the way Ms. Chambry would lean against the window? She'd be backlit and the afternoon classes could see right through her blouse?"

We nod, we remember. She taught eighth grade health and I guarantee we learned more from her after lunch than she ever put on the syllabus.

Freddy stands up on tip-toes, trying to see around the upgraded roofline. "Damn," he says, "they totally blocked the view of the girls' dorm." He sits down beside me and asks, "Remember when we used to come up and scope out the college girls as they changed clothes?"

Since we're speaking of boobs, I think.

"Oh yeah," chokes out a smoking Rick. "Winter was the best. Dark early, curtains open, babes having pillow fights in their bra and panties."

It's my turn to choke on my smoke as his words assault me with an image from some porn we watched a million years ago. "Right," I say, "and then you delivered pizza to them and they didn't have any money and…" My words devolve into a fit of snorts and sniggers.

"Oh my god," Stoney says. "What are you guys? Twelve?"

Without missing a beat, Rick grabs his crotch and says, "Twelve inches."

"Doesn't the foil chafe?" Stoney asks straight-faced.

It takes a second, but then we all melt into a puddle of laughter.

This is the most mellow I have felt in a very long time. I'm very glad I came. "This is nice," I say, retrieving the joint. "I'm glad we did this." I pull myself up to standing and clutching the rail I stretch up and howl, "Happy power!"

"What?" Stoney asks.

I feel a certain freedom being able to talk about my sister. I had no idea how much I missed her. "Allie and I used to watch Scooby Doo together. I loved Shaggy, of course," I snicker, nostrils snorting smoke, "but she loved Scrappy Doo. I didn't even think he counted as a character, you know? I mean, can you say 'ratings baby'? But Allie loved Scrappy Doo. He had this catch phrase and she would go around the house saying it."

I think back to Saturday mornings, she in her Care Bear pjs, me in my shorts and tee shirt. We'd eat cereal on the living room floor in front of the television. I was eight years older than her. At twelve, I was three times as old as she ever got to be. I clear my throat and focus on my story. "Allie used to shout, 'Happy Power!' But the line was really, 'Puppy Power'." I pause and sigh. "It really bugged me." I turn to look at them. "You know? How sometimes the little things bug you the biggest? So one day, I corrected her." I can feel my eyes go glassy with regret. "I broke that little girl's heart. My mom was so mad at me." A laugh catches in my throat. "What's wrong with happy power?"

"What?" Rick asks, eyes glazed.

"Nothing," Stoney says, shaking his head. "It's a good thing." He reclines, stretching out along the flat part of the roof.

"Happy power!" Freddy shouts in a spot-on version of Scrappy Doo, his fist punching into the air.

This brings a smile to my face. *Thanks, guys*, I think. I sigh and shake my head when Rick offers me the joint. "Well, this was great guys, really, but I should probably

151

think about getting going." My mother. This day. Allie. Home.

"What? No!" Rick says, also rising. "Come on, we're not done!" He stubs the fatty into the rail ledge and then drops it into one of his khaki pockets.

I look at him and shrug. "It's been fun—"

"Yeah," adds Stoney. I hear his tendons pop as he extends his arms over his head. "It's been real, it's been fun—"

"It's been real fun," Freddy finishes.

"It has been fun for some, but not for all. It's my turn to have fun," Rick says through gritted teeth.

"You have got to be shitting me," I say. "Come on, Rick, let's call it a day. Seriously, man." I'm shaking my head as I go to pass him on the way down the fire escape. "Fun," I mumble in disbelief.

He slams me against the railing so hard I almost lose my balance and topple over the side, two stories down.

"What the fuck?" comes out much louder than it should have.

Stoney moves in between us, shielding me from Rick and freeing my passage down the steps. He's careful not to touch Rick, but his presence is very known.

The marijuana buzz is DOTR, dead on the rooftop. Rick grunts and turns his back on us till we've all passed and are descending the steps.

This is not the end, we've not heard the last from Rick, but for the moment, I'm safe and feeling content.

152

6:35 p.m.

"Thanks," I say, chucking Stoney on the shoulder once we're driving again. "The castle is just what I needed. Sorry for freaking out," I add.

He nods and I am overwhelmed with relief to be spending this day with him. Funny that some kid three months younger than me is my father figure. That reminds me, "Tell me about Bailey."

Stoney breaks into a broad grin, his proud papa face. "She's amazing," he says. "It's weird, you think you know who you are, what you're capable of, then you have a kid and it all kind of shifts into perspective."

"I know who I am," Rick states. "And I know what I am capable of. And," he pauses for emphasis, "it's my turn to put things in perspective."

C'mon, man, I think. How can he take paternal pride and twist it back around to the murder club? Gang.

Ignoring Rick, I ask, "What's she look like?" I meet his eyes in the rear view for a split second. "I mean, as I remember, Andrea was quite the Betty."

"Hey," Freddy says, "where're we goin'?"

"I'm heading back to Rick's house unless someone directs me otherwise," Stoney says as he flips down his visor, removes a stack of photos and passes them over his shoulder to me.

"Not Rick's house," Rick says.

I thumb through the one-hour photo prints; six snapshots from birth to current, I assume. She goes from squishy-faced, squinty-eyed scowl to bright blue-eyed, gummy-smiled cherub. Like baby Allie. Too much. I choke on my words as I say, "She's adorable, Stone. Happy, healthy. Whatever you're doing, you're doing it right."

He takes the photos and returns them to their place of honor. "She's got Andi's smile," he says.

"Who gives a fuck?" Rick screams, just missing Stoney's head as he slams his hand against the visor. "Don't turn here. We are not going to my house."

Stoney passes that street then puts on his blinker and pulls into a deserted gas station. Old pumps with rotating numerals long rusted in place. The metal plates on the sign show a corroded, sagging seventy nine cents per gallon.

Throwing the gear into park, he says, "Fine, Rick. Where are we going?"

6:39 p.m.

There is a meaty pause, then Rick demands, "Drop me off at the Amoco on Chamberlain."

"Seriously?" I ask. "You bailing?" *Good*, I think.

His head snaps around and he glares at me. "Just drop me off."

"At the Amoco?" Stoney repeats. "On Chamberlain…?"

Silence.

"Okay." He pulls out onto the road and turns left on Heritage to cut over.

"And then I need you to meet me at SundCast."

"SundCast? Like the old factory?" Stoney asks wonderingly.

"The one we already drove past?" I ask. "Twice."

"So, now you know where it is," Rick sneers. "In the back there's a parking lot that you can't see from the main road. You'll have to take the frontage road to get around. Back there, that's where we'll meet. I need you to drop me off at the station and then drive straight there. Wait for me."

I can see the wheels turning as he gives us the instructions. This must've been percolating in the back of his head all afternoon. The anger is subsiding, he seems energized yet again. He's got a plan. I am both intrigued and petrified.

"How're you getting there?" Stoney asks.

155

"Never you mind," Rick says with a cruel smile. "I've got a plan."

See, I told you. In my head I hear an evil laugh, *muah haha*, and I see him rubbing his hands together maniacally. Or perhaps twisting the ends of his long greasy mustache. Something predictably evil.

Obviously, I'm not the only who thinks this, because Freddy, as Vincent Price, lets out a deep and frightening "muah haha haha" and a tremor runs through me, the hair on my arms rises atop goose bumps.

I look at him and we both shudder dramatically, which makes us laugh. Of course, Rick does not see the humor in our actions, but I think he has an appreciation for the intent. His cruel smile widens.

We drive on in silence for a few minutes when I suddenly ask Freddy, "How'd you know to go to the forest preserve?"

Freddy grins to himself as he watches the passing countryside. "I summer camped there every year from fifth grade through twelfth."

"What?" I ask incredulously. "I never knew! Did you guys know?" I look to the front seat, meet Rick's glance and Stoney's in the mirror. Both look surprised.

"So, Stoney's a dad, you had a sister, and Freaky Freddy went to camp," Rick says. "The surprises are abundant today."

"Yeah," Freddy continues as if Rick hadn't spoken. "Remember, I'd go to my rich aunt's in New York every summer?" We all nod. "It was a lie. I was really at camp that week."

"Summer camp? At Grandview Preserve? Why would you lie about that? I don't get it," I say.

He is still smiling to himself. "It was a special camp," he says tightly, making quote marks with his hands. "For poor kids. Poor ethnic kids." He laughs a sour, dry laugh. "We camped on the far east side of the park. At night a few of us would sneak out and explore. After seven years, there isn't much park I'm not familiar with…even after all this time." He smiles nostalgically, his gaze adrift.

"Anyway," he says, snapping back, "there were always these yuppie hikers coming into the park. Did you know Grandview has the only forest preserve to feature granite and limestone quarries? That it's home to over three hundred miles of hiking trails? Or features one of the deepest natural lakes in the Midwest? No, of course not." He chuckles. "Things you grow up with, you take for granted. They lose their importance. Locals don't care anymore, but hikers come from all across America to trek our woods." He shakes his head. "Crazy."

"Yeah, but how'd you…ya' know, *know*?" Rick asks, honestly intrigued. With his strategy planned, he's got more confidence, less dickiness.

Still wistful, Freddy says, "I figured I'd run into—" His smile broadens widely. "Sorry, no pun intended. I figured we'd find some privileged hiker. Someone from out of town. Someone alone, on foot. Nature freaks are a solitary bunch. Someone wealthy. I had no idea how wealthy, though." He's beaming. "That was just a bonus," he snickers. "A big bonus."

I look on in awe as Freddy returns to gazing out the window. I catch a glimpse of Rick, his face strained, the switch flipped, before he moves out of my view.

"I just didn't think you had it in you," I say with awe.

We ponder in silence, I imagine we are all considering what Freddy has done, who Freddy has proven himself to be. Not a Freddy I would have ever guessed.

"Yuppie fuckers," Freddy grumbles under his breath.

We nod in agreement; he'll get no argument from us.

"Once," Freddy begins, talking to the window and the passing landscape of downtown, "this one guy, some a-hole dickhead from Vermont—" His face pinches and his voice alters to an entitled rich white guy nasal, "South Burlington, you know, cheerio, hup, hup." He bangs his forehead on the glass and grinds in the greasy circle. "Me and some kids from camp were out gathering kindling and this guy saunters up to us and asks what we're doing here. Arms laden with sticks and branches and he wonders what we're doing here."

I can see his breath fog and recede.

"What are *we* doing *here*, like he's the only one worthy of the woods. It's fuckin' woods, man."

Just as I'm thinking, crap, he's crying, I see Freddy swipe angrily at a tear. He keeps his face turned from us as he says, "Guy told us we didn't belong there. Said if he'd wanted to see ghetto kids, he would have gone to the Bronx. Then he laughed." Freddy releases this horsey braying sound and I get it. Just hearing that laugh makes me want to run over the a-hole dickhead yuppie.

I punch him in the shoulder and tell him he's been holding onto that for a really long time. "Let it go, man," I say.

He meets my eyes with a cocked head as if to say, *Oh really? You're one to talk.*

Freddy shakes his head at me then returns his gaze through the window. A laugh breaks in his throat as he says, "That's how I learned about the hiker pockets, though." He bounces his head on the glass, then continues, "This asshole proceeded to go through his collection of pockets, zippers and pouches everywhere, looking for some change to toss at us. *At* us. You know, cuz we were beggars." He shakes his head. "Standing there with armloads of kindling, this guy feels the need to call us beggars. He never did find change, but he did throw a granola bar in our direction and mention how tonight we'd dine like kings."

"What a jerk," Stoney says, and we all nod.

Our contemplative ride is punctuated by Kriss Kross and *Jump* on the radio. Whiggedda-whack, indeed.

"Sorry about using your car," Freddy adds, to Stoney.

Before Stoney can reply, I say, "Oh, yeah, we need to do something about the grill. I checked for damage, the hood has a dent and the bumper, too, but I think that's old," I add. "But there is definitely some—" I clear my throat, then continue, "—some evidence. The grate is cracked pretty bad."

"Shit." Stoney sighs. "Well, shit."

"Sorry, man, really," Freddy says. "Shit."

Glancing over his shoulder, Stoney says, "It's an old car, seen its share of adventures. We'll figure it out." Stoney, ever pragmatic.

Rick is grumbling about "four hundred dollars' worth of damage."

"Yes!" Freddy pipes up. "I can pay for the repair work," he says, thrusting his fistful of crumpled dollars into the air.

The Amoco Rick requested is all the way on the other side of town, far, far from the forest preserve and a good hike from campus. Good for us, though, the time driving is like intermission between the events of this crazy day.

"But you always came home with nice clothes," Rick says suddenly.

We all look at him. "What?" I ask.

"Freddy," he explains, "he always came back from his rich aunt in New York's house with nice clothes."

"Oh, yeah," Stoney laughs. "Remember when you both had the same Ralph Lauren Polo shirt?" He punches Rick in the thigh, and still laughing, says, "Rick was not happy about that. Same color even."

"It was part of the camp experience," Freddy says. "A full-service camp, you might say. They couldn't keep us all week, providing a roof over our heads and food in our bellies, and then send us home in a t-shirt that says, 'I went to Grandview Pity Camp and all I got was this lousy t-shirt.' They had tons of donations." With a sniff, he adds, "Might've been your mom that donated, Rick. Maybe she bought two of everything that year and I got half of it. It's almost like we're...*gasp*...twins!"

Stoney pulls into the Amoco, just in time, I think. Rick shoots Freddy a look that confirms my thought. Distracted by 'the plan', he lets go of whatever comment was curdling on his tongue and instead directs Stoney to the east side of the Pantry.

"Now what?" Stoney asks.

Rick releases his seat belt, opens the door and jumps out with a bounce. "Now, we let the master show you how it's done." He stands, then ducking under the door frame, he looks in the car at our wondering faces. "I told you, drive to SundCast and wait for me." Then he reaches under the seat, snatches an object and shoves it in the waistband under his shirt.

"Hey!" yells Stoney, leaning over the gear shift to the passenger side. He is met with a slamming door. We watch as Rick jogs into the gas station pantry.

Peering at us from between the front seats, Stoney asks, "What was that? Was that a…"

We look through the side windows to where Rick disappeared just a moment ago. Sitting in the car, leaden by disbelief, we stare at the reflective mirrored window of the Amoco store. Rick is gone and all we see are three blurry stunned faces staring out of an idling car.

Stoney puts it into gear and pulls out of the lot. He is driving sluggishly, his acceleration equal to his thought process, slow and methodical.

"It was a gun," I say simply.

"A gun." Stoney rolls the word over his tongue, not daring to swallow or spit.

A gun.

"He's insane." This from Freddy, the most recent of our club killers.

"Insanity is in the eye of the beholder," Stoney says cryptically.

"No," I say, "insanity is in the hand of the gun holder."

"Maybe he won't use it," Freddy says.

"Yes," replies Stoney dryly, "because the goal today is *not* to kill someone."

"Okay," Freddy says, "but guns are messy. Guns leave a trail. This is crazy."

"This whole day is crazy," I say. "Pull over, man, lemme in the front seat." I look to Freddy for front seat approval, he nods, used to the rear.

We're cutting back across town, back the way we've already come. *Déjà vu*, I think. *Deja view?* We're stuck on the Jetsons' space treadmill of repetition compulsion, continuously echoing patterns of performance, searching for an exit. *Jane, let me off this crazy thing!*

"He's nuts," Freddy says. "I mean, I'm worried about him. Really worried."

"Rick?" I ask. "C'mon, Fred, he's just...Rick."

"Prince Richard?" Stoney injects with a smile.

Prince Richard was a nickname we gave Rick a long time ago. But never to his face. It was an inside joke because we shortened it to—

"Prick!" shouts Freddy. "Oh man, I totally forgot about that. I don't know how I could have forgotten about that, but I did."

We share a laugh and it feels good. Lightens the mood, but only for a minute.

"Is he doing coke?" I ask.

There is a long pause, seems no one wants to answer my question. Finally, it's Freddy who replies with, "Worse."

Worse? I think. And then I know. "He's dealing."

7:12 p.m.

The shadows are longer this time as we approach the empty manufacturing park. It seems like we've been in the car forever.

"Where do you think he got a gun?" I ask distractedly.

"Probably belonged to his dad," answers Stoney. "He seems like the kind of guy who'd have a whole collection."

"Yeah," I say, "I bet they're in his first floor office. All those years, we were never allowed near that room." I lower my voice and say, "Upstanding is not one of the first words to come to mind regarding the Harris family. Underhanded, maybe…"

"I dunno," Freddy interjects. "I bet it's just the one and it's probably not registered or anything."

There's something about the way he says it that makes me suspicious, but I don't press.

"Ya' think?" asks Stoney, his voice trailing off.

"You're probably right," I concede. "That would explain why Rick would risk taking it. If it can't be traced. That dirty wanker."

"Wanker!" Freddy shouts. "It's like, how much more black could this be? And the answer is none. None more black," he says in a Brit-perfect tribute to Nigel of the band Spinal Tap.

"Maybe," Stoney begins, "we should have stayed at the mansion and watched movies. *Spinal Tap, Die Hard, Spaceballs*—"

"How many assholes do we have on this ship, anyway?" Dark Helmet asks.

"Instead of, you know, what we did," Stoney finishes.

"How mundane," I tell him. "All the cool kids are starting clubs."

"Gangs," Freddy corrects.

I think we each consider laughing at this, but none of us does.

"And I think we're probably the assholes," I say.

Stoney pulls onto the access road that leads to the factory. *When you turn into the lot, the road forks.* We veer left as instructed, around and behind the oversized, sprawling plant.

What a shame, I think. Wasted space, squandered opportunities, and crushed dreams. Something like twelve hundred people out of a job. It really hurt the surrounding towns when this facility closed.

It really hurt my family, I remember coldly. My stepdad worked here. And then he didn't. And when he didn't work, he had all the time in the world to get drunk and take out the woes of his pitiful life on his wife. And child.

I wish I was wearing a watch so I would know how many hours are left of this day. Yes, I realize that midnight, tomorrow, next week, or even next year, won't make things better, won't bring Allie back, but damn, I hate this day.

Stoney pulls up close to the building. No one can see behind the building from the main road or access lane, but

164

somehow it feels safer to be hugging the structure. We park the car and get out, the slam of the doors echoing loudly.

It's hot and humid and dusty. I stretch my arms over my head and look around. There is a whole lot of nothing back here. I see a lower level entrance nearby with steps leading down and a brick stoop built around it at ground level. I sit on the wall and stretch some more, not really touching my toes, but going through the motions. It feels good. Something snaps, or crackles, but definitely pops. *Getting old*, I think. This day has been what—forty? Fifty years long?

"How'd he know about this place?" I ask.

Freddy clears his throat, swallowing loudly, but doesn't speak.

Stoney kicks a rock that skitters across broken pavement and scatters several more tiny pebbles. It's very quiet back here. Not comfortable quiet...lonely quiet. Desolate.

"Freddy?" I ask. "What do you know?"

He shrugs noncommittedly and says, "He meets people out here sometimes."

"People? For what?" I look around. There is literally nothing here.

"Kickball," Stoney says. "Whiffle ball? Red Rover? It's Rick, who knows. Who cares."

"So, what do you think his big plan is?" Freddy asks.

"This is the most I've ever heard you speak in your natural voice, Freddy. Why?" Stoney asks.

Wow, I think, *it's true*. All the time I've known Famous Freddy, he's always been somebody else. Sometimes it drove me nuts, sometimes he impressed the hell out of me, but mostly I just expected it. I can't believe I didn't notice he was using his own voice. A little distracted, I guess.

Freddy is looking at Stoney, really looking at him. "I asked you for the car keys at Futterman's as myself. When I realized I had an idea, me, Freddy, I had a plan that I needed to commit to. I didn't want to hide behind someone else, not even just their voice, when I did...what I planned to do." He shifts his gaze from Stoney to me, then to the ground. He scuffs some weeds with his tennis shoe.

"Wow," I say, eyeing him intently, "that was deep." I'm serious.

"I know," he says, continuing to look down.

I glance at Stoney, when our eyes meet, he nods. Our little Freddy is growing up.

After a reflective pause, Freddy asks again, "So, what do you think Rick is up to?"

"You are never going to believe what happened to Rick..." I continue in a low and ominous voice, "Rick Harris woke up this morning, thinking it was like any other morning, but what he didn't know was..." I swallow a chuckle as I try to restrain my humor until the punchline. "...overnight, as he slept soundly, he was kidnapped by aliens." I nod emphatically. "That's right, in his barbiturate slumber; Rick was abducted, restrained, and probed. Every orifice, some twice, in and out, in and out—"

The other two interrupt with laughter but I gesture *not yet.*

"And finally, after hours of insertion and extraction, through the magic of alien science, Rick was able to stick his own head in his own asshole." The last words of my story come out in a sputter. "And that, my friends, explains a lot." I erupt in laughter, and encourage them so do so as well.

"He does have some bad breath," Freddy offers in appreciation of my story.

I imagine a circular Rick. Instead of the snake eating itself, it's a flexible Rick inserted in himself.

"But seriously," I say, humor abating, "I figure he's planning on carjacking someone with that gun of his and bringing them out here, although carjacking doesn't exactly meet the requirements." *Requirements*, I think wryly, *another punchline*.

"Not in the doctrine," Stoney adds.

"But that's probably where the gun really comes into play." *Play*, another anomalous word in today's repertoire.

"Seems risky," Stoney says. "Witnesses, you know. Gas station on that side of town, people might notice. People might recognize him. They might remember."

"And cameras!" interjects Freddy. "I bet there're security cameras. Lots of 'em. With gas prices so high, I bet they're really paying attention for theft and stuff."

We consider in that manner for a while longer. Stoney comes and sits on the ledge by me. Freddy is wiping dust and grime off the factory windows and peering in.

It's hot. And humid. Windy, too. The dust blowing in from the farmlands is sticking to my damp skin. Gritty and itchy. I wish I had a Coke. Should have picked one up at the Amoco Pantry. That's when I remember the stick of Doublemint and dig it out of my pocket. The green wrapper is soggy and when I remove the foil, the gum bends with warm pliancy. I fold it into my mouth and enjoy the burst of mint and saliva.

I fluff my shirt against my chest, trying to force a breeze, my fourth grade teacher's scientific logic be damned.

"Whew, I really do stink," I say. I could've bought a t-shirt at the Amoco, too. I imagine a commemorative tee that says, *We started a Murder ~~Club~~ Gang and all I got was this lousy T-shirt*.

"Yeah," says Stoney, tossing a worn chunk of glass at me. "I didn't want to say anything, but you are rather odiferous. Considered offering you my car air freshener for a quick wipe down."

We all gag as Freddy raises my arm, takes a big whiff and faux faints with an "Aye yi yi."

There is more dust swatting and pebble kicking.

Freddy picks up a broken piece of cement and begins banging rhythmically on the metal rail. Bam-bam, bam-bam, bam-bam. Right on cue, we all join in on the next round shouting, "We will, we will, rock you!"

I scrounge up a smaller chunk and join him as Stoney slaps his hands on the bar. We run through the chorus a couple of times then launch into the lyrics. Come to find out, once we get past Buddy playing in the streets gonna be a big man someday, we don't actually know the words. Butchering the lines screws up our banging rhythm and we dissolve into laughter. It feels good. Loud and deep and good. Freddy Mercury may be offended, but I think Buddy would understand.

7:30 p.m.

After a few long, relaxed minutes, Stoney asks, "Remember that Halloween we TP'd his neighbors?"

"Of course," I say. "We were ninjas that year. Dressed all in black, we snuck into the gas station to steal the toilet paper, just to see if we could, and when no one caught us, we thought we were so badass. Like stealth assassins."

"TP assassins," adds Freddy.

Stoney straightens up and sets his jaw. "I do believe it was the Wilmer-Farmington the Fourths trees that we assassinated." Relaxing, he continues, "They were so pissed. So stuffy and proper. Their beautiful mansion disfigured by floating streamers of Charmin." He chuckles at the memory.

"Wouldn't have been so bad, but it rained later that night," I say.

"What did he care?" Freddy asks. "He had his staff clean it up anyway. It didn't affect him at all."

"Yeah," I say, "but it got all clumpy and stuck in the branches. Was a bitch to get it all down. It was kind of gross." I laugh. "That was a lot of fun, though."

"You know, if it hadn't been the good stuff, it may have just dissolved. Cheap paper does that," Freddy comments.

"Single ply," I say, nodding. We know about cheap toilet paper.

169

"Ha!" Freddy bellows as a fresh memory strikes. "Remember that health assembly we had in eighth grade?"

We think, then nod, as recollection dawns on our faces.

Stoney breaks into a toothy grin. "The one where I went on stage and brushed my teeth? Crazy, man."

"Yes!" shouts Freddy, enjoying this moment. "And Rick went up there to test strength and agility with Laura O'Keefe." Laughing loudly, he continues, "Man, she made a fool out of him." This is obviously a memory Freddy deems worthy of savoring. I guess it is a good one for Rick-bashing.

I snicker and think, *every once in a while, life is fair*.

We had this health and safety assembly at the middle school. The speaker would ask for volunteers and then select them by student support through applause, holding his hand over each kid and waiting for crowd reaction.

Stoney was chosen to do a teeth brushing demonstration. There weren't many candidates for that one. Seriously, why would anyone brush their teeth in front of an audience? I couldn't believe when I saw Stoney's hand rise. Brushing your teeth? In public? Yuk. But Stoney took the stage, brushed, rinsed and spit into the portable sink they provided on stage. All on film! They had a video camera set up for the assembled masses to see up close and personal. Then he chewed one of those magenta tablets that cling to all the areas you missed. Remember those? They petrified me. I was afraid my whole mouth would be pink, either from the blood I drew from the radical brushing I had given *in public*, or the lack of proper brushing ever. He chewed that tablet quite thoroughly and smiled big for the camera.

I remember a collective gasp echoing through the crowd. There was no pink. None. Only gleaming white, freshly brushed and obviously well-tended teeth. An "oooh" pass through the audience.

Even knowing Stoney as most kids did, this was an impressive feat. I think the announcer was equally amazed. He recovered well and changed his tactic midstream to convey the benefits of proper brushing habits versus the detriments of not being thorough.

That was the same assembly that brought Rick and Laura to the stage. He was a strapping young athlete in the day, ahead of the growth curve for most eighth grade boys. Kickball was the game and Rick was the God.

The guest speaker had needed two volunteers, a strong specimen and a not so strong one. Rick was the solid participant and 'petite' Laura was the other. Funny how contemporary political correctness infiltrates memory. She was a runt. Stunted with short legs and short arms and no neck. The emcee had refused to say weak, even though that was exactly why she'd been nominated. Of course, that's probably because he knew how the demonstration would most likely end.

He'd lined up the two volunteers side by side, a blushing moment for Laura, I'm sure, being partnered with Rick. Then the host had handed them each a feather. He told them to place the feather in their right hand and extend their arm straight out in front of them. That's it. We watched from the safety and discomfort of the gymnasium floor while runty little Laura "Good Grief" O'Keefe outlasted the furiously sweating and obviously weakening Rick Harris, heir to the throne that is Harris-ville.

There was some message in the demonstration about strength not equaling fortitude, or some shit like that. I don't

171

remember, and you know, it's not important. What's important is the message that the entire school learned that day.

"Don't fuck with Laura," I say with a chortle, the other two joining me. We shake our heads, looking off into the past. It's an okay place to visit, but I wouldn't want to live there.

Stoney interrupts my reminiscing, "What are we doing here?"

I'm reminded of my earlier pondering. "Why are any of us here? Not in an existential way—"

Freddy gives me a cock-eyed look. "Huh?" he asks. Then, "Whatever. We should be in an air conditioned place, sitting in front of a television watching," he glances at his yellow and turquoise Swatch, "Home Improvement." He barks out an, "Arh arh arh."

"What time is it?" I ask.

Freddy gives me an exasperated look and in a female voice says, "Does everybody know what time it is?"

I shoot him a quit-fuckin'-around look and shrug. "No," I say.

"Time for Rick to get his ass here," Stoney responds.

"It's Tool Time!" Freddy says, obviously disappointed in our lack of participation.

"It's nearly dark," I add.

"Almost eight," replies Freddy. "Eight o'clock! Shit, a whole day. Man, this is fucked up. Should've just slept in today." He shakes his head, his dark hair flopping in and out of his eyes. "Be here by noon," he mocks in a falsetto version of Rick's voice.

I play with a piece of rubber I found on the asphalt. There is comfort in the pliancy of it. It's warm and well-worn. I stand up and toss it. It sails a long way before hitting a crack in the pavement and taking a funny bounce. "This reunion was totally fucked up," I say. "We put the 'men' in mental."

"We put the 'ill' in Illinois," offers Freddy.

"And the 'nity' in insanity," adds Stoney.

Both Freddy and I turn and stare at him. "What?" is said in unison. When Stoney shrugs with that goofy grin of his, we all bust into hysterics.

I pick up another piece of parking lot debris, but this one is stiff and crumbles when I try to flex it. I chuck it to the side and say, "This has been a domino kind of day." The moment of humor has passed, I'm waxing philosophical now. "You know what I mean?"

Stoney says, "Yeah, man." He doesn't look at me as he continues, "That first thing happens and it knocks into the next. One thing leads to another, to another, to another, and you can't stop it once it's in motion. There're a series of individual events, but they're really a whole. The domino effect."

"Life is like the domino effect," I say. "Sometimes you set up, sometimes you're set up, but eventually it all goes down."

"Whoa, deep," Freddy says. "It sounds cool, though. I like the way you think, kid," he adds in his best Humphrey Bogart. Himself again, "Maybe I can use that for the name of the club." He grins broadly. "Wouldn't that just beat all? If Rick didn't win, and I did!" That giddy squeal again. "I'll

173

teach that…asshole…" He looks to us for support or condemnation and receives neither. We don't care.

"Domino Club? No, Domino *Gang*. Domino Dudes? Domino Nation…" He wanders off, talking to himself, content with himself, proud of himself.

After a few minutes, he wanders back, still mumbling.

"C'mon guys, give a little help. This is hard! What do you think? It's going to be your club, too. Don't you want a cool name?" He is pleading with us, discovering he is not used to such decision making power and he hardly knows how to handle it. "At least I'm asking you. You know Rick won't care what you think," he ends with a falter.

"I just don't know why he thought a gun would be a good idea," Stoney says.

Shit, I think. "What if Rick fucks it up and we get busted? He's the only one without an 'official membership'." I make air quotes. "And the only one who can afford legal counsel."

They both look at me, then at each other, then away. Obvious avoidance. "What?"

Stoney sighs and stares at the ground, rubbing ruts in the gravelly dirt between stoop and parking lot.

When Freddy starts whistling, I have to ask again.

"What?" Stoney meets my eyes and I say, "I know, I know, things have changed since I've been gone. But c'mon, man, things don't really change."

"We gotta tell him, Fred."

The whistling stops.

"Fine, I'll tell him," Freddy says.

"After everything we've been through today, what could possibly be so hard to tell me?

"Rick is poor," Freddy says.

I start to respond humorously, but the expression on their faces kills the joke in my throat.

"No, really. He didn't want us to say anything, heck, he doesn't want *us* to know," Freddy says.

"You know his mom left, right? They're getting a divorce? Well, shortly after that, the Harris Investment Firm was investigated. The assets frozen, the staff cut loose. Bad shit, man." Stoney pauses. "His dad's in jail."

I can't believe what they're saying. "But—"

"No buts, I'm telling you, he's broke."

"The house, the car, the wad of bills?" There is a grin plastered to my face by disbelief, waiting for the punchline.

"He's up to his nuts in debt. Owes favors to a lot of bad people."

"The fuck you say?" falls out of my mouth before I can even form the sentence in my head.

"Oh, it's so much worse than just drugs," Freddy says, his voice dropping off. He sits beside me on the stoop ledge, too close for platonic relations, this must be serious. I want to move over, but I don't. "Michelle…she kind of went off the deep end after her mom left." He hunkers in even tighter. "Took the fucking dog but not her daughter." He shakes his head, so near, I feel the wisps of his hair. "Michelle got into the drug scene. Bad." He looks away. I can see the knot tightening in his throat. "She," he chokes it down, "she got scooped up by a guy named Brody."

Stricken by the absurdity of it, I laugh out loud. "Brody? Sounds like a member of New Kids on the Block."

With absolute seriousness, Freddy says, "Trust me, he's a very bad man." He swallows hard, the words thick. "Brody is short for Bro Daddy. Big, bad, mean motherfucker. He's a dealer and a pimp. Michelle, she—" his voice cracks and he tries to regain composure with a wrenching throat clearing. His Adam's apple bobs with the effort and he grimaces. "Michelle was hooking to pay for her habit."

"What?" I ask, my voice rising. I stand, backing away from the covert circle of confession.

"Yeah," interjects Stoney. "Rick had to buy her back. It was really…ugly."

"No way." I shake my head, thinking back to my meager exchange with her poolside. She looked like crap, that's for sure. But upon further reflection, her hair, her pallor…and were those track marks? "Fuck."

"Fuck is right," Stoney says. His shoulders sag as he stares off into the dusty distance.

I'm having a hard time wrapping my mind around this. "Poor Michelle," I begin. "How'd he," I stammer, "but if Rick—" I falter again.

Stoney starts to say how things have changed and I silence him with a glare. "There's change," I shout, "and then there's having your entire fucking world turned upside down."

"Says the guy who initiated the murder gang," Stoney says quietly.

"Sometimes I run for him," Freddy says. He is still sitting, shoulders slumped. "This lot back here, this is where we make some of the exchanges."

"Oh, Freddy." I'm shaking my head. I don't know if I want to hug him and tell him it's okay or slap him upside the head and shout *what the fuck*? "Okay," I say, "so…what? He's still in the house. Got to be stuff he can sell."

176

"Done. Sold what he could. Sold what the banks didn't take."

I begin pacing, my mind is a whirl of thoughts. "What about school?"

A gruff sound erupts from Stoney's throat. "He conveniently forgot to mention during his rant that he got kicked out months ago. Just because the semester recently ended doesn't mean he just got home."

Home, that word again. My whole life it seems that as soon as I think I know what home is, the welcome mat is yanked from beneath me.

"They've been slacking around that house living on Mountain Dew and delivery pizza."

Freddy snorts. "Not like Michelle eats."

"It's only a matter of time until the bank takes the house." Stoney shakes his head. "I don't know what they'll do then."

"Might be in jail by then," Freddy says. "Or dead."

I run through what I know, what I remember about Rick and his family. "Grandparents? Aunts? Uncles? Anybody?" Words tumble out even as I mentally discount them. "Country Club friends?"

"You mean those cunty cohorts?" Freddy says snidely.

My head keeps shaking. *No, no, no.* The very foundation of all things Rick is based on the knowable truth that he is wealthy. Privileged. Agree or not, believe or not, support or not, he is of the entitled. In another time, place, or person, I might think this was fair. "Karma," slips out of my mouth.

Freddy nods, he gets it. "Maybe."

"I kind of figure today is the first day Michelle's gotten any natural vitamin D in months," Stoney says. "I think she's trying. Trying to be normal. Whatever 'normal' is anymore."

"So…how desperate is Rick to make a big score with this murder club thing?"

"It's not even about the money," Stoney says. "I think he needs to regain some of his Rick-ism, you know?"

We all nod, we know. Prince Richard, he needs to rule. To be in control. But how far will he go to regain his stature?

Genuine concern sets in as we hear a car approaching. It's coming fast over broken road, hitting potholes and spitting gravel. Anxiety and doubt cloud our faces in anticipation of a situation none of us can predict.

"Ruh-roh," Freddy says as Scooby Doo, and I wonder, are we the meddling kids? Or are we the monsters revealed?

8:37 p.m.

We all jump to attention as the car careens around the back of the building. A nice car. The closer it gets, a *very* nice car.

Rick is in the passenger seat. The man driving looks awful. Frightened, wide eyed and frantic. Rick on the other hand looks ecstatic. He is the boss. He has never felt better, stronger, more content. In this moment, he is truly happy. I don't know that he's ever been happier. Ever. It's almost as if he's been waiting his entire life for this opportunity. And it shows. A pre-murderous glow.

The BMW comes to an abrupt stop about twenty feet from where we stand, the tires gripping firm despite debris. I see the glint of the barrel before I see the weapon. *My god*, I think, *he's actually got a gun*. Even though we knew he had a gun, I still didn't really believe it.

Rick screams at the driver to get out. He looks at us for adoration, aren't we proud of his authority? The guy gets out, foot catching on the floorboard of the door. As he is righting himself, Rick yells again, "Hands on your head!" I am surprised he didn't add 'faggot' or 'asshole' to his command. His hands shoot to the top of his head before he has fully regained his composure. He wobbles awkwardly until he can recover his balance.

Walking around to the driver's side, Rick takes this action either as defiance or inferiority and reaches out a gun-toting hand to swat the hostage nastily across his shoulder.

The guy barely maintains standing, his knees buckle and he cries out, hands still firmly on his head. He straightens and stands as still as possible, whimpering softly, refusing to make eye contact.

"Good dog," Rick says cruelly.

My mouth is suddenly parched, my tongue thick with the words I want to shout. The gum that brought me pleasure is a dry and tasteless trespasser. I spit it out, wishing that I could remove myself from this situation as easily.

Rick's victim is wearing a t-shirt and running pants, tennis shoes and what looks like a red and yellow striped slap bracelet on one wrist. I think he's probably thirty, maybe a little older, it's hard to tell. He's been crying, dirty streaks stain his face. A silver line of dried snot connects his left nostril to his cheek.

Rick is moving forward, motioning toward the Beamer with a wave of the gun. "Nice, huh?" He's grinning. "What d'ya' think?" He nods, his mop of hair slapping his forehead. "Sweet ride," he says, answering himself.

"Very nice," says Freddy coolly. "But cars don't count."

"Shut up." Rick points the gun at Freddy and fakes the click of cocking.

We all flinch. We're watching, wondering. Waiting.

"Okay," Rick screams at the guy, "fun's over." With snorts and screeches from his nose and throat, his hyena-like laughter is on the verge of manic.

The guy is muttering. "...mistake, mistake, big mistake..." His voice quavers, his breath hitching. "...not my car, not me, mistake…" His hands are on his head. His whole body is shaking. His nose is running again.

"Rick," I say firmly, "what are you doing? This isn't a torture contest. What's the point?" I'll admit, I'm kind of freaked out right now. Never the most stable of the bunch, Rick is carrying a gun. Holding it like he knows what he's doing, too.

"Shut up," he says, pointing the gun at me this time. Even though I was expecting it, I still wince.

"Quit pointing that fucking gun at us," Stoney forces through clenched teeth.

"Where'd you even get a gun?" I ask, trying to distract, maybe diffuse this situation.

"All in due time," he says, circling his prey menacingly.

"Not me…mistake," the guy babbles over and over. Snot is running freely from his nostrils, mixing with saliva, bubbling on his lips.

Rick tells the guy to "SHUT UP," emphasizing with pointed gun. "I'm going to shoot you," he states. "Then I'm going to rob you. Guy like you driving a car like that must have a nice little sum in your wallet. In your *pocket*," he corrects himself, eyeing the three of us. His gaze focuses narrowly on Freddy, but he speaks to his victim. "And it better be more than four hundred dollars," he adds caustically.

At this moment, the guy's eyes roll up into his head and his muttering becomes more insistent. "Not me, not me, mistake, you don't understand, it's a mistake, a mistake, not me, not mine…"

"Shut up," Rick says again.

The guy gets louder, the words rushing from his mouth. "Listen!" he screams. "I've got nothing! No money! Not my car! Fucking boss says, 'Hey, Michael, I know it's your day off and you're in the middle of a racquetball game, but could you take my car to be serviced and fill it up for me *right now*? Misty and I are heading out first thing in the morning and you know how *I hate to do it myself*!" He is shouting, droplets flying liberally from his wet face.

It all comes out in a flow of words and splatter coasting on a wave of bitter laughter. He's exhausted himself and hiccups as the last of it escapes. His body is still standing, hands on head, but his spirit is broken. Regardless of Rick's intentions, he has accomplished total and complete annihilation of this man's soul.

"What?" asks Rick icily, rubbing the barrel with his hand, caressing it, stroking it with purpose. He is on the verge of exploding; this is the calm before the storm.

My brain screams, *Alamo!*, even though we've surely never had a Rick tirade such as this.

We stand there wide-eyed, mind and bodies on edge. Every last nerve tingling. Afraid to exhale and possibly trip his hair trigger.

"Rick," I begin, but I falter. I've got nothing. He shushes me with a wave of his hand. The other hand.

"What?" he asks again in a voice I barely recognize. "What are you trying to tell me?"

The guy takes in a deep breath. It's quite an effort. "I told you," he says with complete resignation, "it's not my car." His chest hitches and a cry escapes. "I've got no money, no credit cards, no fucking lottery ticket. I put the gas on his account. I was playing racquetball for Christ's sake." Another wet catch of his breath. "I've got nothing."

BOOM.

Stoney, Freddy, and I all jump. We'd been fixed on the guy, hanging on his every word. We never saw Rick's arm rise, we never heard the cock of the gun. We never sensed the pull of the trigger.

One second, we're watching this guy, next thing there's a ruby bullet hole above his right eye and a splattering of squishy matter flying out the back of his head. It lands with a squelch on the pavement behind him. He crumples to his knees, hands still on his head. A look of surprise on his face, as if he isn't quite sure what happened. I imagine we all share that expression. Finally, his body tumbles to the side and hits the ground with a *whumph*. Dust flies up around him like a shaken rug. Momentum rolls him onto his side, exposing the back of his head, or what used to be, for all to see.

Freddy immediately gargles bile from his already emptied stomach. He stumbles, barely three steps away from us, before something catches and it sounds as if he is dredging up remnants of meals long forgotten.

"*What the fuck!*" Stoney screams at Rick, hands flying into the air, his paralysis broken.

I stand rooted to the pavement. My senses raw.

Rick dives in and begins fumbling through the guy's workout pants. Again and again. The flimsy mesh liners inverted and lying loose on the dead man's hips. He is slamming and tossing the body up and down, flipping him over and back again, checking for a possibly missed pocket.

183

Somewhere, anywhere. There are none. He's mumbling about "hidden fucking Freddy pockets."

Rick grabs the waist band firmly, jerks and rips the pants loudly apart at the seams. Still holding the torn material in his fists, he begins punching the guy's torso. Punching and punching, the filmy shreds looks like handlebar streamers, as he continues to wail on the guy. The body barely registers the pummeling, the fists bouncing off the gym-toned body.

Rick staggers to his feet. He shoves each fistful of cloth into his pockets and starts kicking at the already battered body.

In a total immersion of sensory overload, I am very aware that Michael, the racquetball player, lackey to the boss, and witless victim of Rick, has shit his briefs. With a sudden attack of immaturity, I am stricken by inappropriate, twelve-year-old sniggers made worse by the heavy silence.

Rick turns to me, fists clenched, breath fast and heavy.

"Sorry, sorry. It's just—" I'm trying to speak while choking back untimely laughter. "You beat the shit out of him!"

I hear Stoney groan long and loud.

Rick has the courtesy not to crack wise at my comment. He wipes an arm across his face, smearing a hot day's worth of sweat and grime and frustration. He nearly loses his balance, trip-hopping over the body and spinning away from us. His arms and legs are shiny with perspiration and I can see bits of dust and gravel sticking to him.

"Put him in the car," Rick commands in a tight voice.

I don't know why, but we do. We comply as if Rick is Pavlov and he's just rung a bell. Well, Stoney and I respond to this conditioned stimulus. Freddy makes himself scarce, hiding behind Stoney's car until the deed is done.

Grabbing arms and pantless legs, for the second time today, Stoney and I help dispose of a body. We take great effort in keeping his head facing up and even greater effort to not look. Carting the dead guy to the car, we prop him up in the driver's seat, reclining it slightly so his limp body can work with gravity. Stoney places the seatbelt across him, fastening the clasp then jerking it tight to lock it which helps hold him in place.

I close the door to this ninety thousand dollar car, that is not his, and we walk over to Stoney's piece of shit vehicle that no one would ever kill for.

Freddy is waiting. His pallor mimics the rising moon. Waning, shadowed, and with a dire expression stamped there.

The three of us get in, saving the shotgun seat for Rick, and watch as he walks casually to the BMW, unzips his shorts and pisses on the window separating him from what is left of Michael. He zips up and ambles around to the gas tank. Taking the remains of the nylon pants from his pockets, he rips the light fabric into strips and ties the ends together. Then he forces one end into the gas tank. He wipes the gun down with the edge of his shirt, holding it in clothed fingers as he shoves the barrel into the hole to secure the polyester strip before stretching the rest out across the parking lot. It's about a twenty foot wick. Rick removes his trusty lighter and touches the flame to the very tip of the material.

Sprinting to Stoney's car, he yells, "Let's go!"

185

Stoney has the car on, in gear, and ready to roll. We pull out of the lot the same way we came in, only quicker this time.

A barrage of thoughts ricochet through my head. I'm wondering, *what just happened? Will it burn? How fast? What if it doesn't? That fucking Rick.* Of all my scatter of thoughts, the one that rings loudest is, *that fucking Rick.*

9:31 p.m.

We do not speak as we drive. The a/c hums and pings as it works overtime to cool down a car overheated by elevated emotion. We've driven about a mile when we see a burst of flame followed by thick black smoke, but no sound. The mushroom is funneling into the sky, backed by the azure and crimson line of a deeply setting sun.

"What'd you do that for?" Stoney demands as he thumps his hand against the steering wheel. "You could have gotten us killed!"

Personally, I am disappointed that there was no whoosh or rattle, no push of the car from a big wind caused by the explosion. No additional wave of heat. No big bang. All we see is the thick black smoke roiling upwards.

"Yeah," I say, "that was not necessary…at all."

"Not to mention the big giant arrow you provided for EVERYONE. 'Hello, crime being committed *RIGHT HERE*'," says Freddy making alarm sounds in his throat while pointing emphatically with his finger. Anger seems to have replaced his nausea.

We all jerk as the delayed sound of an explosion catches up to us.

Rick continues to stare out the side window. He is not acknowledging us. I think he'd like to deny the whole damn day. Even though I've called him an asshole at least a dozen

187

times today, and meant it, I suddenly feel sorry for him. Poor guy. No mother, no father, no trust fund. Can't even kill a guy without making it into a production. What a major disappointment he must be to himself.

Spoken words seem to be the enemy of contemplation. In quiet, we process. Stoney is glaring fixedly at the road. Rick is watching his side view mirror, although with distance and darkness, I doubt he can see anything. Freddy has his eyes closed with his head pressed to the glass. I am just the observer.

Life is a fuckin' science project, I think. This day would make a perfect case study. *Youth of America, the fine line between child, adult, and recklessness.* It seriously depresses me to think that I am missing a golden opportunity to start my dissertation. Because we'd all go to jail. *Honest, officer, I was just collecting metadata.*

The cop cars, fire truck, and ambulance pass us, lights flash but no sirens blare. We're still on the outskirts of the city, not much traffic and no stoplights. I wonder if they know what they are rushing to. I can't imagine they do. Won't they be surprised? The sight of emergency vehicles begins to bring Rick out of his stupor.

"Can you imagine the theories that will be flying around about this fire?" he asks.

Interesting that he doesn't mention the murder theories.

"Mob hit? Drug deal gone bad?" Rick ponders aloud. "Disgruntled boss?"

"Oh, I guarantee, he's disgruntled now," Freddy says.

As we enter town, I notice that Stoney takes a roundabout way back to Rick's house. I bet he's avoiding any unnecessary remembrances of today's path of events.

188

I say to Rick, "How'd you get a gun?" It's not a question so much as a demand.

He shrugs, his gaze never wavers. "I got connections."

Freddy explodes, "What the hell have you gotten us into?"

Rick turns, and in the glow cast from the dashboard equipment, I see him scowl. "I didn't get you into anything. You made me do this."

A rich boy's defense, all of the entitlement, none of the blame.

"Don't worry, you pissant fagbag," Rick says to Freddy in a low tone, "I got my ass covered. You better hope you do, too." He rotates back to his front-facing position.

Freddy and I exchange a look of bewilderment, *what the hell?*

Stoney slams on his breaks and steers to the shoulder of the residential road. "What," he shreiks, "is that supposed to mean?" He quiets his voice, white-knuckled hands gripping the wheel. "You better not be fucking us over, Rick. We go way back, share a lot of history. If there's something we should know, you better tell us."

"Fuck. You."

"No, really," I say. I'm getting nervous. "C'mon, Rick."

"Nothin'," Rick states. "It doesn't mean anything. Come on, let's go." He sags into the seat, shrinking. "How could this happen? How, how, how?" He shakes his head back and forth. "I planned it out so carefully."

So carefully? I think. *What? Since noon today?*

Rick slaps a hand on the dashboard and we all jump. We're on edge, preparing for a break-down or blow-up. I am extra thankful that the gun is gone.

Stoney pulls back into traffic and begins driving again.

Rick says, "I waited through half a dozen potential marks before that guy showed up. Seriously," he looks back at us to convey his gravity, "I passed over a Lexus, an Escalade, and two Mercedes!"

"What was your plan?" Stoney prompts.

Rick smiles. "It was a good one." He relaxes a bit, leaning into the headrest. "It came to me this afternoon. Just came to me!" He snaps his fingers and the smile widens. "I'll stake out a gas station, that one specifically because of the clientele." He snorts. "Rich, careless, above common crime. My dad went to that Amoco." He laughs but it breaks mid-breath and comes out as a cackle. "I bought a Mountain Dew, you know, to make it look like I have a reason to be there. I'm standing by the magazine rack, it faces out the front window, and I pretend to peruse the selection while I stalk potential victims." He pauses here, introspective.

Freddy sits forward to ask, "What about security cameras? And witnesses?"

Rick bites back his first response, sighs, and addresses Freddy's obviously ridiculous question. "I go there a lot. Anybody saw me today has seen me before. Me and Amy, the clerk, we, how should I say this, we investigate the back alley occasionally on her break. I buy her cigarettes; she fucks me and tells me company secrets. Like the fact that the cameras are for show. No film, or video, or whatever the hell they use now-a-days. Shit, if you look close you can see they don't even have wires. Not even connected."

Freddy leans back, content with this answer and maybe a little impressed despite himself.

190

Eyebrows up, look of *can I get on with my story?* on his face, Rick continues, "When he pulled up in that car, I just knew he was the one. Great car, man, nice fucking car." He sighs. "When I saw him in work-out clothes, I thought of Freddy's hiker. I thought, jackpot! Cha-ching." He grabs an invisible slot machine handle and cranks downward.

He's staring between the seats, not at us, but in our general direction. He's telling us his story, but he's really detailing it again for himself. "Casual clothes," he continues, "nice car, filling up for a summer getaway of debauchery." He shakes his head slightly, still unbelieving, checking for the error in his plan. "Debauchery costs money! And cash equals no paper trail. I'm golden, I think." He suddenly looks around, meeting our gazes one by one with an expression of desperation. It's getting really dark out, but there's no mistaking the look in his glassy eyes. "I'm golden," he states, recalling that sense of triumph. He will continue his tale to ultimate woe, but at this moment in the story, he is golden.

"When I see him hang up the pump, I head for the door. Feeling so clever as I hold the door for his entry and then pass him on my way out. I saunter up to the passenger side of his car, like I belong there. I open the door, slip inside, close the door. I even put the seat belt on!" Rick is mostly talking to himself, but we listen intently.

"He must've been distracted returning to the car because he didn't even notice me 'til he was getting in. That's when I showed him the gun. 'Get in,' I say and I smile real nice." He shows us how he smiled for the guy. Not nice. "Turn on the car and head west on Chamberlain. We're going for a little ride."

191

Rick turns towards Stoney, "I was so smooth. My voice was calm and authoritative. I was riding high, man. I loved it." Eyes unfocused again, he continues, "He starts to resist, so I cock the gun. Instant compliance. So cool." His head bobs. "We ride in silence for a few minutes—me still smiling, him working the situation through in his head. Finally, he says, 'You've made a mistake.' I laughed at him! Laughed!" He repeats loudly, not laughing now. "The guy says again, 'No, really, a mistake.' He tries to make eye contact with me then and I shove the nose of the gun into his shoulder. 'Road,' I command. A few minutes pass. Again he speaks, saying, 'What do you want?' I tell him I want him to shut up and drive."

Rick turns to face forward, relaxing in his seat. "I start fiddling with the stereo. Nice car like that, you know he has a Bose. I'm scrolling through the stations when he asks me, 'You want the car? Take it, just take it. I don't care!'" Rick says wistfully. "No wonder." Hindsight illuminates like the first rays of dawn. A dry chuckle. A toss of the hair. "Again, I tell him to shut up. I find a classic rock station and crank it up. *Boom, boom, out go the lights*. Who did that?" He looks at me, resident musicologist.

"Pat Travers," I reply.

"Oh yeah," he says vacantly. "Rocks, totally rocks." He punches the roof and yells "Boom!" and we all jump. "Boom," he repeats, then, much quieter, "out go the lights…"

Still bobbing to the song in his head, he says, "I look over and I see this guy is crying. Crying and praying to god. 'Our father,' he begins, and I think," he spins to look at Freddy, "c'mon, Freddy, what am I thinking?"

"Our father, who art in prison?" answers Freddy tentatively.

"Ha! Good one!" Rick laughs, then says, "But no. I smacked him and said, 'I am your god.' Then I called him some choice names and put the pistol right to his temple." He takes his fingers and presses them straight to his head. He seems to be enjoying this reproduction of power.

"'Shut up,' I say. Then he's blubbering and his nose is running and Donnie Iris comes on the radio with, *Ah, Leah*, and come on guys, you know I love that song!"

We do. When Rick was fourteen he lost his virginity to his tennis coach's seventeen year old assistant. Her name was Leah. She lost her job.

Rick is animated again, as much as the seat belt will allow, anyway. "The guy is still mumbling, I can see his lips moving. I scream at him, SHUT UP, and I totally crank the tune. He cries harder. So then I'm screaming AH, LEAH and beating on the dashboard and do you know what that fucker does?" He looks around at our faces. "He pulls over! Right onto the shoulder." He is absolutely floored by the gall of this guy.

Shaking his head, Rick says, "Went from sixty to zero in about fifteen seconds. They never show that part of the commercial, but braking is just as important as accelerating. Man," he says, waxing with admiration, "that was one sweet ride."

Rick's shaken out of his reverie by his own next comment. "Then he is screaming at me! 'Just take the goddamned car!' he yells. I shut off the radio." He shows us with a twist of his wrist, although I bet it was a push button. Rick looks at me and Freddy in the backseat and continues,

"I stare at him and calmly say, 'Shut. Up.' He starts to unbuckle his seatbelt and I have to shove him back into the leather upholstery forcefully with my left arm while I wave the gun in his face with my right. We both sit warily. Finally, I tell him to get us back on the road and open this baby up. I don't want your damn car, but that don't mean I don't appreciate it!" Rick cracks a smile and chuckles.

"This asshole is so confused, he has no idea what's going on. He does as he's told and pretty soon we're topping 110, 120, 130. So cool." For a moment, Rick is lost in the exhilaration and admiration. "He handled that car like a dream. Under duress! That says a lot. Then we turned into the industrial park. And the rest," he sighs, "you know." He keeps shaking his head from side to side. "How could it have gone so wrong?"

For the first time that I can remember, Rick is truly beaten. And not like with the feather assembly, this is the most human side of him I've ever seen. On the heels of a botched robbery and overly successful murder, Rick is almost...humble. Almost...likeable. How sad is that?

And just like that, *finger snap*, it's over.

10:16 p.m.

"Hey!" Freddy yelps suddenly. "I win!" Laughter erupts from his lips, filling the car uncomfortably. Freddy has never been known for his social skills. He's never been the life of the party, the king of conversation—or even the prince. Except for comic, his timing has never been on, and this behavior could not have emphasized it more.

"Ha!" He sits up, straining the lap belt, and beats the back of Rick's headrest. "I win!"

"Freddy," Stoney says sternly, "not now."

I give him a routing elbow to the ribcage, guiding him back to his seat. I narrow my eyes and shake my head curtly. "Where to, guys?" I ask.

Freddy sits back into his seat, his butt scooting back with jerky little movements, but I can tell he doesn't want to. Ignoring my question, he says to me, "You always think you're so much better than us."

His comment takes me by surprise. "Huh?"

"You don't think I notice how you look at me? Like I'm a bug in a jar? It's not just me. Rick and Stoney, too." He leans in as I pull back. "You're a very judgey kind of guy. You think you're keeping it to yourself, but we notice."

Freddy's face is in mine and his voice drops in an accusatory manner. "The silence, the smirks. We may be specimens, but we're not blind."

195

"Freddy, I—" I begin, but he cuts me off, which is good since I'm not sure what I thought I was going to say.

"You analyze and identify and try to categorize us, to label us in your college educated mind." He returns to his side of the back seat and offers in the matter-of-fact voice of Freud, "Eet's a deestancing mechaneesm. You suffer from illusory superiority."

The shock must be obvious on my face.

"What?" Freddy snaps. "I took Psych 101." His gravitas breaks. "Twice," he finishes, then laughs.

"Wow," is all I can muster. Of course, it's true. I do observe them and am always running commentary in my head. I'm doing it right now.

I meet Stoney's non-committal glance in the rear view mirror as Rick cough-sputters *head case*.

"Today has been very enlightening," Freddy says. "For the first time, I feel like maybe, just maybe, we got to see behind your curtain."

I don't know what to say, so I don't say anything.

With the rant over, Freddy's mood quickly bounces back. His eyes are bright as he says in a sing-song voice, "I-I wi-in." I think he'd like to dance. Jump around. Flail his arms and do cartwheels. I'm thankful for the restraining belt.

"Take me home," Rick says.

"What?" Freddy asks incredulously. "I thought we were going to celebrate?"

"Nothin' to celebrate," grumbles Rick, staring out the side window.

Freddy is exasperated. "That's not fair," he cries. "If you'd have won, we'd be celebrating."

196

"This whole thing was stupid," Rick mutters. He seems to catch his own reflection in the dark window and doesn't like what he sees. To Stoney, he says, "Take me home."

Grumpily, arms crossed, Freddy says, "Aw, let's not just go home. I don't want to go home…"

"It's been a long day," I interrupt. "I'm exhausted." I am. Mentally, physically, emotionally, I am toast. I barely remember walking into Rick's house this morning. It seems a million years ago, a million miles ago, a million memories ago. I was a different person then. I did not change willingly. Or did I? I catch myself, I'm doing it again. But at least it was me I was analyzing. *Illusory superiority*, huh.

Ding, ding, ding.

"Shit."

"What?" I ask Stoney.

"Tank's on empty."

"Stop at the Mobil, I'll fill you up." Freddy has never offered to pay for gas before.

Maybe it's a ploy to delay our next decision or maybe Stoney really is concerned about driving on fumes, either way, he pulls into the station. Freddy shoots a wad of bills between the seats towards him. I don't see any hundreds so it must be the diner cash.

I hop out and grab the squeegee. First I clean the windshield on Rick's side, then I drag the dripping sponge along the grill. Can't hurt, might help. I dunk repeatedly in the filthy blue liquid, *take that forensic evidence*, then wipe the driver's side window and slosh the front panel again.

Stoney runs in to pay and we're back on the road. The whole digression took less than ten minutes. Not enough time to alter the mood in the car.

"Maybe we should all go to Rick's for a while," Stoney suggests. "I think we have things to discuss."

"Nothing to discuss," says Rick, head resting against the window. I see his breath fog the glass for a moment, clouding his reflection, then gone.

"No, Stoney's right," I add. "C'mon, Rick, some serious shit went down today. We need to make sure we're all on the same page with this."

"I think we could use some down time." Stoney continues, "I think we need to...decompress."

"Yeah," adds Freddy. "What's that called after a military expedition? You know, after a mission they have to...ah...something..."

"Debrief," says Rick shortly.

"Debrief?" questions Freddy.

"Yes. De-brief."

And Freddy snickers. An honest reaction, real and pure and instantly I know that he is thinking de-brief as in underpants removal. He has been pantsed enough in his lifetime to truly appreciate a word like 'debrief'. His mood is infectious and pretty soon, we're all sniggering. Even Rick.

I wonder how they'd react to my earlier vision of mental debriefing, but I don't share. For the moment, things are okay.

We all laugh a bit more and it's as if the very air inside the car has been filtered, ionized of all negativity and is suddenly breathable. The atmosphere relaxes and even though the hilarity has died down, the normalcy remains. We continue on in silence, destination: Rick's.

10:28 p.m.

When we arrive at Rick's house, the mammoth structure is all angles and foreboding shadows from the 'safety' lighting. These mansions are fitted with security systems that rival military bastions. Theft at this level is all white collar, anyway, so I don't know why they bother. Because it looks cool, I guess.

I don't think anyone is home. Not many options, I guess, since it's just the two of them. Michelle's sporty little Mazda Miata is not in the drive and I feel the need to ask about her.

Rick's jaw tightens. He releases a deep breath and says, "Can't lock her in her room."

We head back to the pool house. The air has cooled with the falling of night, but there is a dampness that continues to hang heavy. It still feels thick and I think I smell rain on the breeze.

It is here, in the gloom of the evening and dramatic shadows cast by the security lights, that I notice the things I should've noticed sooner. Like the shattered bricks on the garage and peeling paint of the pool house. The previously immaculate lava paving is sparse and intermingled from no replenishing or tending, like a rocky reimagining of a Pollack painting.

The door jamb to the pool house is splintered and I wonder why someone would need to kick in the door. I realize the imported Italian tile has spider webs of cracks and there is grout missing. Was I so caught up in the past that I missed the clues that were right in front of my face?

Unlike earlier in the day, we gladly open the fridge to share an alcoholic beverage or two. Rick grabs the first round, popping off bottle caps at the counter and pinning the three opens to his chest with one arm as he swigs from the fourth.

Bottles, of course. Import, as if there were any other. I'm thinking *old habits die hard*, as Freddy says, "Knock off a liquor store lately?" to which Rick answers with a devilish, "You know it."

I don't know what to know.

We proceed to the living room area this time. I fall into the middle of the sectional and sink comfortably within the soft cushions. I grunt with contented satisfaction. Running my hands over the textured fabric, I notice it is spotted and crusty.

I am tired, so tired. I need a pillow and a place to use it. I'm not picky, too drained to care. I would gladly curl up amongst the crust crumbs and sauce spills right here and crash. *I don't even need a pillow*, I think as the headrest conforms to the back of my head. I sigh deeply and my eyes flutter closed.

I'm jolted upright by the press of a cold beer to my cheek. "Not yet," chuckles Rick, as I lurch forward with a start, and an expletive, before accepting the icy bottle he is offering.

I yawn and sit up. *Not yet?* I throw back a long swig of Heineken. The wetness refreshes me as I feel the cold swallow travel from my mouth, down my throat, through my chest, to my stomach. I feel the kick of the alcohol almost immediately. "Whoa," I utter involuntarily. That's the difference between Bud Light and imported draught. Heady, hearty, full bodied—it goes straight to my head. I smile, relaxed.

Stoney sits down to the left of me, on the wing seat of the sectional. He holds his beer with reverence, seemingly deciding whether to imbibe or not. I mentally will him to do it. *Take a sip*, I press with my gaze, *it will do you good.*

Freddy pulls the suede ottoman to the side and sits on it with a snort. I think he expected more resistance than his ass met with. The furniture may be worn and stained but it's still quality.

Freddy's bottle is practically empty already, probably not a good sign. If I can feel the buzz after a single swig, I worry about the potential static in his head. Like I mentioned earlier, I've never known Freddy to be a competent partier. He's a lightweight all the way.

Rick sits to my right, on the arm of the sectional. Not the most comfortable spot, especially for a guy used to so much comfort, but it gives him height over us and that's more important. I guess comfort is subjective.

Poor Rick, I think, *always struggling with dominance.* As the firstborn son of Richard William Covington Harris II, his entire life has been preordained. His decisions do not matter. His successes do not matter. His failures do not matter. All of it, entirely irrelevant. He is a continuation of, drum roll please...the line.

Although he has always strived to be something other than The Third, or at least he thinks he has strived, his insurgence has been met with expectations. He may have rebelled against societal and familial expectations, but that's exactly what someone in his position is supposed to do. Therefore, rebelling is actually conforming.

Rick is spoiled and resentful. And everyone knows it but him—he is a cliché. Every action and/or reaction he has ever participated in has been lifted directly out of the *Rich Kids Book of Entitlement*. Rick knows how his life will play out, where he'll end up, regardless of his intent. And that, my friends, is why Rick is a dick.

But wait, I think, *maybe the game has changed*. He may still be a dick, but for different reasons now. He's never had to work or try to excel on his own. The real world, or at least the world he currently finds himself in, may eat him up and spit him out. *Welcome to the curb, buddy*. Already he is showing signs of deterioration. Is it too late for him to learn coping skills?

Illusory superiority, I think and a groan escapes on the heels of acknowledging what I shall call my *Freddy Christened Complex*. I need a twelve-step FCC program.

"I need a cigarette," I say.

Rick fishes a pack out of one of the khaki pockets and tosses it to me. It's weightless with only one or two cigarettes remaining. He flips open his lighter and it takes several flicks of the flint wheel to catch. Even the Zippo is exhausted.

It's the best inhale of the day, and I exhale slowly, savoring the smoke in my lungs. With my buttless hand, I rub my fingertips lazily over a small tear in the seam of the fabric. "Hey," I say, "remember Stoney's VW?"

There is a mutual bobbing of heads as grins appear.

202

I pull back on the thread, revealing sofa cushion stuffing. Fingering the fluff out through the hole, I pick and pull at it like a magician's never-ending scarf. "Remember how we had to use beach towels to cover the seats because there was no upholstery?"

"The driver's seat had upholstery."

"Yeah," Rick says knowingly, "and the passenger seat was okay. But the backseat frame was exposed like the vulture-pecked bones of that sad little vehicle. Could've been on display in a museum."

"Ha!" Freddy cries. "The car-cass. I remember it well."

"The good news was that if we ever road-tripped on the fly to the quarry, we were fully stocked with towels," I say. True story.

"But then we had to sit on wet towels," Freddy says, grimacing.

"Hey," Stoney says, "if you had a problem with my bug, you could have walked."

"Could've probably walked faster," Freddy says as Fred Flintstone, before making cartoon feet running sounds and pedaling his sneakers in the air.

"And there was only one handle for the inside!" I shout with abrupt recall. "We had to take turns rolling down the windows."

"Oh, that's right! Do you remember—" Freddy shouts.

"Alamo," grunts Rick.

"—when Rick got locked in the car because we took the only crank?"

"Al-a-fucking-mo," Rick growls. "We've all heard the story, we all remember the story, shit, we were all there when it happened. Let it go."

Freddy snorts, trying to withhold his humor, which makes him laugh even harder. "But…but…" he sputters. "It was so funny!" He mimes rapping on a window and mouths, *Goddamn it, lemme outta here!*

"Cut it out, guys," Stoney says. "It's been a long day. Let's drink our beer and settle down."

Freddy feigns yanking on a car door and slips to the floor in silent hilarity.

10:56 p.m.

"You really have to buy your sister back from a pimp?" I ask unexpectedly. My bottle stops on the way to my mouth, equally surprised at my outburst.

"What the fuck?" Rick's beer hangs midway to his lips, too. His gaze swings angrily towards Freddy who is getting up to get another beer.

Freddy offers an Alfred E. Neuman, *What, me worry?* grin, then motions with the empty bottle, "Another round?"

Rick clears his throat. "Michelle had incurred some debt," he says tightly. "I took care of it."

"Yeah, but—" I begin.

"Ran into your mom the other day," Rick says, interrupting me. The bottle finally reaches its destination and he takes a deep drink.

"Beer?" Freddy calls from the fridge.

"Was real nice to see her. *Real nice.*"

Now, it's my turn, "What the fuck?"

Freddy returns and places four beers on the coffee table. I notice the dust that coats the tabletop, interrupted by rings of bottle perspiration, crumbs, and the skipping trail made by a spinning beer cap.

Freddy pops his cap with the bottle opener and begins chugging. On a different day, this might strike me as odd. On a day like today, I almost expect the unexpected.

Rick finishes his beverage and drops the bottle. It shatters loudly, sending emerald shards across the floor. He reaches for a new bottle as he stares at me the whole time.

"Yeah, your mom, man, she's hot. Pretty. Hot. And tempting…a PHAT mess," he says, slamming the lid on the edge of the table. Overflowing foam forms puddles among the glass remnants. No wonder the place looks like shit.

"You little mother—"

"Fucker? Hey," he taunts, "how'd you know?"

"Shut up, Rick." It's Stoney, he sounds tired.

"Aw, c'mon, I'm just—"

"Really, shut up." Stoney sits up a little straighter and sips his beer. "We need to talk about what happened today."

That's when it hits me. I may not be the fastest train on the track, but when the realization dawns, I am up and off that sofa and shouting, "Goddamn it, Rick, if you gave my mother drugs, I will fucking kill you." I drop my cigarette into my almost empty beer, the hiss of the drowning cherry accompanying my growl as I hurl the bottle at his head. He ducks and grins at me as the Heineken missile smashes into the entertainment center at his back.

"Ah, he gets it," Rick says.

I fling my body at his perch atop the armrest. "You asshole," I scream, taking him down with a crash on to the cold, hard floor.

Stoney grabs my arm as soon as I bring it back to punch Rick, so I sit harder on his torso, grinding my ass into his chest. He coughs and sputters, trying to catch his breath.

Freddy helps Stoney wrench me off of Rick. They force me into the corner of the sectional, wedging my knees with the heavy coffee table.

"Stop it," Stoney demands.

"Wow," Rick says, standing and shaking off the assault. "You're mighty strong for a skinny fella."

"Shut up," Stoney tells him yet again. He stands between us, arms out, helping us keep our distance. "We've got enough to talk about without going there."

"Going where?" I shout, my knees banging off the table as I rise. Freddy puts a restraining hand on my chest. "E tu, Fredday?" I ask, falling back onto the cushion. "You know my mom is an addict. You *know*." My voice breaks and I choke down the rising sob. My imploring eyes turn to Stoney. "I stayed with you the first time she went to rehab. I slept on your floor and you read me *Thinner* by Stephen King until I'd fall asleep." I gag on an escaping breath, remembering the times I'd pretend to fall asleep just so he'd stop reading, and then be awake all night with the gypsy horrors reoccurring in my young mind.

"Rick," I plead, "I stayed here the next time and the time after that. I just can't believe—" I'm a mess of emotion, anger, and disappointment, and it impedes my speech. I swallow hard, trying to pull myself together. Freddy hands me a fresh beer and I gulp it down. "I can't believe you'd do that to her. To me." I wipe my mouth with the back of my hand. My eyes burn, my throat, too, as I stifle a gassy eruption.

Rick shrugs. "Sorry, man. If you haven't been told," he glares at first Freddy, then Stoney, "or noticed," he spreads his arms, encompassing the room, "my life kind of sucks."

I don't know what to say. I start to rise again and this time Freddy lets me. "I'm done."

"Sit down," Stoney says firmly, shoving me. He grabs the last beer before moving the table out and sitting down beside me.

Freddy heads to the refrigerator again. "I'm getting another," he states rather matter-of-factly. "One in waiting? You?"

I give him a wave of my free hand. "Sure," I say, thinking I may really need another. Or I really might not. I'm not really sure.

11:10 p.m.

"This was a bad idea," Rick says, shaking his head and draining his bottle.

"What?" asks Freddy stupidly, head in the fridge.

"A very bad idea," Rick states firmly. He sets his empty on the floor amid the remnants of his last. "Shit," he says as if just noticing the mess he's made.

"Oh, ya' think?" This from Stoney, with a sideways glance.

"You cheated," Rick snarls at Stoney.

"Oh," says Stoney with sudden clarity. "The initiation wasn't a bad idea, you losing was." He sips from his bottle. "Ah, I see."

"Shut up."

"Oh, stop," says Freddy, returning with four fresh beers.

These have to be the last, there weren't that many in there.

He practically has to shove the beer at Rick. We all see that his bottle is empty. We all know he wants another. But somehow accepting the proffered beverage from Freddy is beneath him. Of course he takes it, sans any kind of gratitude.

I sit partially forward to grab for mine, swipe the slick sides and flick my hand free of condensation. I thank Freddy with both words and a look. The decline of civilization begins with the ungrateful.

Right, Mr. Psychology, I think and sigh to myself. Freddy's diagnosis continues to haunt me. Mock me. Illusory superiority, my FCC. I have no rebuttal.

Freddy steps around Rick and plops down once more upon the ottoman, this time ready for the ass-acceptance of the cushy seat. He takes a swig, wipes his hand over his lips and says, "You're just pissed because you lost. No," he corrects himself, "it's more than that. You are *fucking* pissed because I *fucking* won."

"You cheated," Rick says under his breath, looking away from Freddy.

Freddy continues unimpeded. "Big, bad, powerful Rick got slaughtered at his own game." He laughs and takes a slow pull from the beer. "That's the only reason you started this whole thing. To make yourself feel powerful. No, to prove how powerful you already were." Freddy is staring directly at Rick, eyes boring into the side of his head as Rick refuses to look in his direction.

Rick continues to take measured sips from his bottle. Looking down at the ground, but still sitting on the arm of the sectional, back straight, shoulders taut, bottle held firmly in a white-knuckled grip. Rick says nothing, but I see deep color blooming upwards from the collar of his shirt. It makes his day-old beard growth shimmer blonde against the maroon flesh.

Maroon, I think. The Hyland Maroons mascot must have been a very angry white guy.

"Haha," Freddy laughs and continues, "it's like in the book, *Crime and Punishment*. You think you are a superman, an uber man, and everyone else, present company especially, is less than you."

Honestly, this is the most I've ever heard Freddy speak at one time. His oral book reports in high school were shorter than this. And in his own voice, too. *Amazing*, I think, looking at him through fresh eyes. This has been good for him.

"Superman!" Freddy continues. "You always treated me like I was less than you and I always believed it. You set the rules, and I followed. Rule number one, according to Rick, rich people are better than poor people. Rule number two, as described by the Rick-ster, handsome guys are entitled to more than average looking guys." At this point, Freddy looks around at Stoney and me, maybe seeking support, maybe trying to figure out if he counts as average looking.

Rick continues with his wayward stare, but it's definitely more pointed. The flush has creeped up and glows hot in his cheeks.

Freddy is on a roll, he keeps talking. "Rule number three," he practically shouts, "as employed by the Rick-o-rama, is the most important. Oh yes, can I have *an amen*?" He is staring at Rick again. This is between them, Stoney and I momentarily forgotten.

"Amen!" he yells in an ethnic sounding preacher voice. "Rule numbah three, my children, is that people like Rick, especially the one that *is* Rick, get to treat everyone who is *not* Rick, like shit." He stops to take a breath, then, once again as himself, "People like Rick get to win all the time, every time, because people like Rick are making the rules." Freddy stands up, stretching to his full height. He seems

211

larger, too, like his confidence has added inches to his slight frame.

"How many times have you cried foul today? Claimed that we cheated?" He swings his gaze purposely to Stoney, then back again to Rick. "Sour grapes, man. Never learned how to lose gracefully. Accept defeat. Welcome to your first life lesson. You're welcome, by the way."

Freddy keeps shaking his head. I think he's just about reached the end of his lecture, but no.

"In the game of life and death," he booms, "I beat you. I win, I win, I win!" He does a crazy little jig, legs dancing in crazy jerky movements. He digs in his pocket, grabs the big bills from the hiker and waves them about.

Something goes flying and clinks against the tile floor before rolling under the table. "Ha!" he shouts, getting down on hands and knees to retrieve the errant coin.

Thrusting it in Rick's face, Freddy says, "Lucky fucking penny! Lucky me," his voice lowers to a methodical taunt and he continues, "I'm the leader of the club, your precious club. I get to give you ord—"

With a vicious slash, Rick whacks Freddy's hand, sending the penny soaring through the air.

I watch, as seemingly in slow motion, the coin flies toward the door, bouncing off the wood and dropping to the floor with a series of delayed tings.

Before the penny has even settled, Freddy's hand comes swinging forward, smacking Rick flush on the cheek. There isn't much power behind it, no resulting rocking of his head or tossing of his floppy hair, but the unexpected nature of the action causes Rick to recoil.

Stoney grabs Freddy and drags him out of the line of fire, shoving him toward the door. "Don't," he says to Rick. "Sit."

Once again on all fours, Freddy picks up the penny and holds it in his fist. He stands and resumes his stance. "What was I saying?" He motions with his free hand in the direction of his empty bottle. "I'm thirsty. I'm the boss. And I order you to get me another drink."

"I'll get it," says Stoney, backing away from the toxic space between Freddy and Rick.

"No," Freddy says through gritted teeth. He's glaring at Rick and the fisted penny bounces on his thigh. "My wish… is Rick's command."

Stunned silence, breath is held, eyes dart around the room nervously.

Rick is up and off the arm of the sectional before any of us can register his next move.

"You want a fucking beer you fucking faggot?" he screams. "Here's your fucking beer!" and he chucks his nearly full bottle at Freddy. With a fortified launch, the glass and its contents spiral the short distance through the air.

Freddy ducks, but the bottle glances off his shoulder with a thud and change of course. It lands on the ottoman, where it rolls, spilling the remaining liquid until it falls, finally finding purchase at the edge of the rug.

"Well, aren't you a wanker," Freddy says, jumping to the side of the ottoman. He raises his fist, but it holds no threat. "Smooth move, Ex-Lax," he continues. "Real mature."

Suddenly the hierarchy has returned. It's as if there's been a physical shift in the molecular structure of the room.

"How come you're above the system?" Freddy cries. "How come you don't have to follow the rules? Huh, Rick? You made the fucking rules." This last part comes out in a whine, raw with emotion.

"I wouldn't have bothered if I'd known you were going to win." Rick spits the words out of his mouth like skunky beer.

"What a life you must lead," Freddy responds, head shaking, shoulders stooped. "Only playing when you know you'll win. Don't you ever just do anything for the challenge? For the opportunity? For the fun of it?" He takes a breath, unsteady but determined. "For all we know, you've killed lots of people. And gotten away with it. Maybe last time, your *plan*," he says this word with an ugly twist of his mouth, "worked great." He's clutching that penny so hard, his fist is white as he says, "Stalking some poor rich sap like that, killing him for fun. Robbing him for no reason. Maybe you act on this impulse all the time."

"It was his idea," Rick sneers, throwing an evil glance my way.

"Maybe," Freddy continues, ignoring everything else, "just maybe, this is how you deal with your daddy issues. How you keep from actually killing him. Maybe you kill by substitution. Maybe you've killed him over and over again." He punches his fisted hand into the palm of the other. "And this was the first time you had an audience for your sick game."

11:17 p.m.

"Good point, Fred," Rick says, shifting his glare to me. "We all know your story now. Maybe what Freddy says is true, huh? Maybe—"

It's my turn to tell him to shut up.

"What was that you said, Fred?" Rick sits up, straddling the armrest and taps his temple. "Hmm, if I recall, you said something like, 'for all we know, you've killed lots of people. And gotten away with it.' What else was there?"

"Stop," I say.

"Rick, don't," Stoney says. Out of the corner of my eye, I see him shake his head sharply.

"Maybe," Rick continues, rising, "you kill by substitution. Maybe you've killed him over and over again. Yes, I think so. Didn't you imply this laundry guy had small-man syndrome? Like your stepdad? Isn't that right? Your stepdad was a tiny little drunk fuck, a weasley wife-beater who—"

I lunge from the corner seat and my knuckles connect with his flapping yap before he can finish his sentence. I half expect Stoney or Freddy to restrain me, but they don't, and I wail on him. Pummeling his face with my fists.

"Like stepfather, like bastard," he slurs between punches and I stop.

215

Oh my god, I think. *Oh my god, no.* I pull myself to standing, using the coffee table for leverage. Shaking off the muscle cramping and raw knuckles, I extend my hand. Rick accepts it with one hand while he rubs his cheek with the other.

"Damn, man," he says, rotating his jaw from side to side. "If I have to drink Twinkies through a straw…" There are streaks of blood crisscrossing his face and chin. His nose is beginning to swell and the flesh around his eye is darkening.

"Fuck you," I say.

"Alamo," he replies, and a round of laughter erupts. We can't help it. If there's a fine line between love and hate, there's also a fine line between truth and absurdity.

I shrug and sigh. "What am I going to do about my mom?"

Rick looks at me, his brow furrowed. "Truce?"

I raise my bruised hands in resignation. "Truce."

"Truth?" he asks, licking blood off his lip with his tongue.

"Truth," I say, nodding.

"She's messed up. Deeper than rehab can reach. Deeper than you can fix. If the only peace she gets is when she's high, let her be high. Let her go. But don't beat the messenger."

"Messenger?" I scoff. "Dealer!"

"Tomato, tomahto."

In that moment, I both hate him and admire him. He probably wishes his parents' problems could be assuaged with a baggie of blow or packet of smack.

"I'm so tired," I say.

"I know," Rick says. "Me, too."

"We're too young for this. To feel like this."

"Are we?" Rick asks. "After today, I think we're all old. Older." He shakes his head. "Shit, I've never felt closer to dead."

Stoney hands us both damp kitchen towels to tend our wounds and tells us to "Sit down."

"Can I talk?" Freddy asks.

"Not yet, Fred," Stoney says. Then to me, "Maybe you should take your mom with you when you leave for grad school. It's been ten years since Allie's death. Maybe she's ready to move on. Maybe," he pauses, "maybe what you need is each other."

Rick nods with agreement.

A chill runs through me. His words slice deep. Mom and me, we are the only reliable thing either of us ever had. We are both running from our pasts, from our poor decisions, from our grief, but maybe Stoney is right. Maybe it's time we ran together instead of apart. "Good idea," I tell him. "I'll talk to her about it." Suddenly, I want to leave. I want to be with my mother, I want to be home.

"*Now* is it my turn?" Freddy asks.

Nobody answers in the affirmative or otherwise.

"Okay," he says, standing, "as your president…Shit, what title did we decide?"

"While you're up, Freddy, I need a beer," Rick says flatly. Just as quickly as his humanity blooms, it, too, wilts.

"Um, no," Freddy replies. "Not that you can't have a beer, just that, well, you're mighty wasteful, Rick." He indicates the rivulets on the ottoman and the remains on the

217

floor. "And besides, get your own damn beer. And get one for me, too."

When Rick doesn't move, Freddy rolls his eyes and shakes his head. "We really should have picked some up at the Pantry. Wanna make a brew run, Rick? No? Okay." Freddy shrugs and continues. "So, as your esteemed leader," he punches his fist in the air, the penny still secured there, "my first rule of action is to say welcome to the club, er, gang."

I can see Freddy's wheels turning. I think he's been rehearsing this speech since he first accepted the challenge of initiation.

With his empty hand, he reaches into his pocket and again withdraws the four one hundred dollar bills. Not so clean, not so crisp, but they still spend the same. And they represent so much more than spending money.

Rick slips a packet out of one of his pockets, pinches the corner and sniffs, first in one nostril, then the other. He still has blood smeared on his face from my beating and the powder clings pinkly. He's lucky to be able to sniff at all through the engorged bridge of his nose.

"Damn," I mutter, amazed at his audacity.

"Want some?" he asks, pinching and sniffing then rubbing his bloody gums with a forefinger. He groans and slides off the armrest onto the seat cushion. "This is the good stuff," he says, "uncut."

"You can't do it, can you, Rick?" Freddy asks. "You can't not be the center of attention." He frowns in disappointment.

"Fuck off," Rick mumbles under his breath.

"No, Rick," Freddy chastises, "you don't have the floor. I do. Me, Freddy, the president of the fucking club. That's right, pre-si-dent of your fucking club. Gang, shit." He runs his free hand through his hair. "How's it feel, Rick? To be a loser?"

Freddy takes tiny steps in Rick's direction, but stays out of arm and leg reach. "Let's see," he says, straightening to face us all, "if we assigned positions by order, I guess that makes you Vice President," he nods at me, "and Stoney would be Secretary, and Rick, well, Rick you got nothing. I guess that makes you not special at all. As a matter of fact, you are officially unspecial." Freddy chuckles.

He's off script and backs up a few steps as he regroups. I don't think he's enjoying this as much as he thought he would.

"So," Freddy says, clasping his fist in front of him, "what now?"

"What now is you all go the fuck home and we pretend this day never happened, that's what now," Rick says with a rush of words.

I couldn't agree more.

"Yeah, sorry, Fred," Stoney begins, "but I think Rick's right. We did some stuff today that probably shouldn't be discussed."

Freddy starts to speak, but Stoney holds up a hand and continues. "I know, I know, I was the one who said we needed to talk about it, but really, after everything that's already been said, I just don't know that it would do any good to say more." He shrugs and looks at each of us. "We had an agreement, followed the—" he shushes Rick with halting gesture, "—rules. We're all equally guilty. I'm cool with it." He considers this, "Well, cool may a severe overstatement, but, you know, I did what I had to do and it can't be undone."

11:28 p.m.

Freddy stomps his foot and shouts, "No, dammit! For the first time in my life, I'm the boss. Me. In my own voice as myself, I won." He drops his shoulders and his tone, "C'mon, guys, give me something."

"I'll give you a boot in the ass," Rick snarls. "Shut up and go home, Freaky Freddy."

"Don't call me that."

"I made you Famous, I can make you Freaky."

"One more beer," Freddy says as he heads to the fridge. "No more beer," he shouts over his shoulder. "A ha, but there's whiskey." He comes forward brandishing a bottle.

"Put that back."

Freddy twists the cap off as he heads to the kitchen to find a glass.

"I said," Rick says through gritted teeth, "put that back."

Freddy continues to talk to himself about being president and drinking whiskey as he opens and closes cupboards searching for a glass. Mumbling, he asks, "Do you not wash dishes around here? Just throw the dirty ones away? How can there be no glasses?"

Rick follows him into the open kitchen, Stoney and I sit at attention. We exchange a glance and rise fully to follow Rick.

Opening another cupboard, we hear Freddy muttering, "Guess I'll just drink from the bottle." Leaning against the counter, he tilts the bottle away to better read the label. *"The right Bushmills is like the right friend."* He looks up at the three of us, all standing, as if in line for a swig from his bottle. "Maybe Bushmills is the friend I've been wishing for my whole life."

He sniffs the liquor, swirling the contents. "You," he motions toward me, "you're like the invisible man. Not here even when you are here. And Stoney, you're the best friend I've ever had, even though, I'm probably like," he hiccups, "the eight hundred and fourteenth friend you have." The next hiccup is deeper and wetter. "Rick," he expels the word, "you are not a friend at all. To anyone."

"Put the bottle down," Rick demands again. He softens, "Come on Fred, it was my father's. It's—" his voice falters, "it's like all I have left of him, you know?"

Freddy's face twists cruelly as he tilts the bottle to his lips and chugs. His Adam's apple is bobbing with the passage of the amber liquid and it burns my throat just watching. He finishes a good quarter of the bottle, wipes his mouth with the back of his fisted hand, and lets out a mighty belch. The air hangs heavy with the scent of whiskey.

"Right," Freddy says. "The house, the car, the sister… those things don't count?"

"Fuck you, they don't."

"Well," Freddy drawls, "I would think that a man with a plan, that man would be you, Rick, a man with a mighty plan, I would think he, erp, would be able to buy another bottle of whiskey." He waggles the bottle. This strikes him as quite funny and he laughs with a big, deep buzzed guffaw.

I don't think I've ever heard Freddy cocky before. Maybe this is how he talks to himself, but he's surely never spoken to anyone else this way.

"See, Rick," he continues, "the difference between rich, good-looking, privileged you, and poor, geeky un-entitled me, is that I learned to do for myself." Freddy emphasizes his autonomy with a tilt of the whiskey bottle to his mouth. "No glass? No problem." He swallows a sip. "Mmm, smooth." Licking his lips, he gestures the bottle in Rick's direction. "See," he continues, "you could learn a thing or two from me. I will make a great leader." He lifts the bottle to take another swig.

Setting his beer on the counter, Rick calmly takes a single step towards Freddy. Then he whacks the bottle out of Freddy's hand, the neck cracking against his teeth. The Bushmills shatters on the floor, more mess for no one to clean up.

"You asshole," Rick cries, as if the wasted whiskey is not his fault. He opens a drawer. We can hear him riffling in there, silverware clanking. Freddy swears and cradles his busted lip.

The lucky penny drops as Freddy catches blood in one hand and fumbles along the counter for a towel.

Rick fingers his drawer prize. In one smooth motion, he withdraws a large knife and surges forward, slipping the blade effortlessly into the fleshy part of Freddy's abdomen. There is a sickening slurping sound as the knife enters and is ripped sideways.

Freddy's groping hand knocks Rick's beer off the counter as it changes course to clutch his belly wound.

The beer foams as it spreads, rapidly running free, seeking lower ground, finding crevices and following grout paths in a geometric pattern. Then there is blood spattering the foam, mixing with the beer. Soon the stream is so heavy, the grout gutters are not deep enough to continue to direct the flow and there is a river of blood. And then a lake.

11:36 p.m.

Rick pulls the knife out with a slick, wet, slurping sound, slopping blood and bits of viscera on the counter and himself.

As Freddy is crumpling to the floor, slowly, wetly, like a tower of sodden towels, he speaks. These murmured words are to be his last. And I don't even know what they are. It makes me sad that I don't know what he said. A man should bear witness to another man's final words. Regardless of what they are, they should be important. They should be remembered.

Rick turns to me and Stoney. Tittering, he shouts, "I win now, right?!" He looks wildly at us, between us, then back and forth. His face covered in drying blood, his eye, nose, and mouth swollen and engorged, he says, "I win! I win because Freddy has at least four hundred dollars in his pocket! Pocket money!" He laughs wildly, the sound ear-splitting, like glass scratching glass. "Plus whatever pittance was his own, but that hardly matters," he babbles, "because either way, I win!" He cackles madly.

Stoney and I stand there, mid-stride, frozen. A million thoughts fly through my brain, most useless is *and the leftover diner cash.* My mind is a blur that burns out just as quickly to complete blankness. I've got nothing. I do not know what to do. I cannot understand what has been done.

And then for some reason it registers—Freddy's last legible words, "Welcome to my Domi-Nation."

11:44 p.m.

Stoney is trying to talk to Rick. Evenly, soothing, in that oh-so-Stoney way.

Rick is not listening. He appears to be the opposite of catatonic. He is a mumbling, bumbling, spastic ball of energy. The knife is still in his flailing hand. It slices through the air, flinging droplets of Freddy's innards, not threatening, simply forgotten in his currently animated and distracted state.

Rick's voice is rising and his words are rushed. I think, no, I hope, that maybe he will hyperventilate and pass out. Or at least be forced to stop and take a breath. Instead, he gets the hiccups, and his lively rant becomes comical with the interruptions.

Stoney is still talking. He seems to be in shock as well. *Okay, Captain Obvious*, I chastise myself, *of course he's in shock*. We're all in shock. Except for Freddy. He's dead.

Fucking Famous Freddy is dead. He couldn't even *almost* survive—not even when his life depended on it. I want to laugh, but I can't. Unfunny. Un-fuckin-funny.

On autopilot, Stoney keeps talking, repeating Rick's name with every platitude. "It's okay, Rick. Slow down, Rick. Have a seat, Rick. Okay, let's put down the knife, Rick. Rick? Look at me, Rick."

Gingerly, Stoney guides him to one of the big, wooden chairs by the kitchen table. He presses him down into a sitting position.

At first, Rick doesn't seem to notice. His resistance is not malicious, just preoccupied. When his butt hits the hard seat, he is jarred out of his psychosis. He stops giggling, blinks rapidly, licks his ragged lips. And hiccups. He tries to rise, his gaze finally focusing on Stoney.

Rick's eyes are steely, his tone suddenly threatening. "Back off," he says.

Stoney restrains him as best he can, still speaking slowly and repetitively. He sneaks a desperate glance my way.

Rick looks around wildly, like he is seeing the mayhem for the first time. "Fuck," he says. Then, "FUCK!" he shouts. "My dad is gonna kill me."

He seems to be assessing the situation. There is a lot of blood, the broken glass and beer slop an ancillary concern. The gore is pretty much confined to the tile by the kitchen counter. There are occasional splatters, but mostly, it's just pooled and drying on the floor.

"Look at all that blood," he says tiredly. "God," he sighs, "why's Freddy such a pussy?" An evil glint sparkles in his eyes. "Ah, but I showed him." He nods to himself, emanating a sick sense of pride. He starts to stand up again, but Stoney continues the pressure.

Rick raises the stained knife, bringing it too close to Stoney. Stoney backs off, warily, releasing his pressure. Rick begins to get up, coming off the chair too fast, too forcefully, again too close to Stoney. I grab his wrist and twist, slamming him back into the chair. It creaks against the tile under the weight and force.

"Put that down!" I scream at him. "Put that goddamned knife down. Drop it!"

Venturing closer, Stoney repeats, "It's okay, Rick."

I am reminded of his Gracie mantra.

Rick's face twists cruelly. He snaps at me, "Afraid I'll kill your *other* best friend, too?" An evil gurgle emerges from deep in his throat, interrupted by a burp. It'd be laughable if it wasn't so totally fucked up. "Don't worry," he says, "his pocket money isn't worth killing for. Don't know why he even bothered..." Rick's voice trails off and I think he may be slowing down, I loosen my grip. He jabs his arm upward, slicing Stoney's forearm in the process, and I again slam him into the chair.

"Shit, man," I scream as Stoney clutches his wound. "Come on Rick, drop the knife." I can't maintain control of his weapon-wielding hand. He's like the incredible hulk. We don't like him angry. His arm is flailing and I can't get close enough to restrain it. He's lost it. Completely mental. This cannot end well. Have I mentioned how I hate this fuckin' day?

With all of his might, Rick lunges forward. A feral scream escapes from his lips. At the last minute I am able to grab his wrist, twisting the knife away from Stoney...and into him.

He came so fast! So hard! I release him, jump back. My hands are up by my shoulders. I'm shaking wildly, my mouth is open, my mind reeling. Rick falls back into the hard chair with a thud, another screech from molded mahogany meeting unkindly with Italian tile.

I'm no medical student, but I can guess that the knife has pierced his heart. There is a steady but thin stream of blood pulsing around the edge of the blade. His hand is still grasping the shaft, but it drops before he can pull the blade free. He looks at me, first with wonder and then with what appears to be fear. Then he smiles. A sweet smile. A kind, forgiving smile. Almost a…thankful smile. His body goes limp and suddenly topples over onto the carnage-coated floor. There is a sick smacking sound as his flesh meets the tacky drying blood.

11:53 p.m.

I stand there stunned. A full minute passes. Maybe ten.
Maybe a million, who knows. What is time? Finally I look at
Stoney. He is off to the side, staring at the bodies.

I start to say *I'm sorry* at the same time that he is saying
thank you. "What do we do?" I wonder out loud.

"Leave," he whispers.

"What?" I am genuinely confused. "We can't leave!"

"Sure we can." He tightens the towel he's wrapped
around his arm and secures it with a chip clip. "It's not so
bad," he tells me, raising his wound. "Pretty superficial
considering." Even through his calm demeanor, I can see he
is trembling.

"We can't just…leave."

"Yes. We can," he replies. "Rick was high, out of his
mind. He killed Freddy. Then Rick killed himself."

I look at him. My mind does not comprehend. My body
is tremoring with waves of shock. That mutant organ I grew
earlier has birthed an entire gutful of mutant babies.

"It's easy," he says with a sigh. "We'd already left.
Hours ago. We have no idea what happened. Or why. We'd
had a really nice day together." With his good arm, he is
reaching for my elbow, supporting me, guiding me toward
the door. "We hung out just like old times," he continues.
"Drove past the high school, had lunch at Futterman's Diner,

scaled the castle building. Just some old friends who met up to reminisce."

I gesture toward his knife wound.

"This?" he asks. "Box-cutter accident. Happens all the time in the stock room."

I look around as I stumble towards the exit. We don't have anything to collect, we didn't bring anything. And when, if, the cops find our fingerprints, it will be because we were here. We have nothing to deny, we have nothing to hide.

Stoney is talking to me in the same tone he used on Rick and I think he missed his calling. Delivering groceries may be his job, business may be his degree, but his career should be in counseling. I imagine him years from now advising his teenaged daughter through a bad grade, a missed shot, her first heartbreak, and her second. He is a good man.

We walk out to the driveway together. The air crackles with an impending storm. Lightning flashes in the distance.

A good solid spring rain will break this unseasonable heat, cleanse the air.

I shuffle over to my car and open the hatch. "Here," I say, pulling the Scooby Doo blanket out. "I want you to have this." I begin to remove the halo from the covers, then shake my head and rewrap it. "You can have the blanket, too. It was Allie's. It's definitely seen better days, but…" My words catch in my throat. *Ten years*, I think, *it's been ten years since she was taken away*. Clarity breaks as I realize I'll never get to counsel her through a bad grade, a missed shot, her first heartbreak, and her second.

I clear my throat and continue, "Take the halo, you deserve it. A gift for your Bailey Angel." I pass it to him. "Happy power, man."

Stoney takes it from me, arm dropping with the weight. "Whoa," he says and we both laugh. "Heavier than I remember."

We stand side by side in silence, both knowing this is truly the end. Of a very long day, sure, but so much more.

He slips his towel-wrapped arm around my shoulders giving me an awkward hug. As he's walking back to his car, he says to me, "You never killed anyone." It's not a question.

My mind leaps to the bodies on the floor of the pool house and I feel my color drain.

"No," he says, reading my pallor. "Not them. *Him.*"

I say nothing and he shrugs in response.

"Then why'd you—" I begin.

He gives me a half smile with very little mirth.

I know why.

"A better question is," he says, "why did they?" He nods to the place where our friends are bleeding out.

No need to ponder. I know their whys, too.

I shift my weight from side to side. My body aches from the repeated surge and purge of adrenaline. Looking off into the darkness, I take in a deep breath, tasting the tang of the impending storm, and hold it. I release it with a cleansing *whoosh.*

Stoney nods. He loads the "O" in his car, sliding it over to the shotgun seat. The open door dings, his shadow long in the light cast from the dome. "Thanks, man," he says. "Just,

233

ah…thanks." There's a pause as he folds himself into the driver's seat. "Go home," he tells me.

And I do.

May 23, 1992

12:01 a.m.

Special Thanks

First and foremost, I must thank my spouse without whose constant support and occasional badgering, this project would not have been completed. A close second goes to the rest of my family who have supported my pursuit of publication. I appreciate your patience, especially during all those times I said, *"Not now, I'm writing!"*

I would not be closing this publication without the help, guidance, assistance, critique, and brilliance of my fellow writers. Thank you DAWGS, RWG, Chicks of the Trade, In Print Professional Writers' Organization, CWA, UW Writers' Institute, Hi-Rev Writers, and DACW, you have all provided me with the tools I needed to complete this, the first of many (!) projects.

About the Author

M F Lamphere, born, raised, educated and residing in northern Illinois, is a creator. I am a writer, designer, artist, parent, and grandparent. (Yes, I take credit for my part in those creations, as well.)

I am a lover of words—both visual and aural, and of people, places, things, images, and beauty in all of its forms.
I'm also an appreciator of the dark side of those things.
I believe there is a fine line between truth and absurdity.

Thank you for reading my story.

Let's hope it doesn't take another forty-nine years to publish the next one.

You may reach me at MFLamphereAuthor@gmail.com

About the Book

POCKET MONEY was the very first novel I completed. And if I'm being honest, originally, it wasn't much of a novel with only a twenty thousand word count. Nearly nine years, much development, and over thirty thousand additional words, it has become a novel I am proud to have indie published.

I hope it entertained you. I hope you got something out of it. I hope it leads to discussion—of both the, "I wonder why the author did this" and the, "I wish the author had done that" varieties. I hope it gets you thinking.

Please like and share the POCKET MONEY Facebook page.

POCKET MONEY

32611660R00154

Made in the USA
Middletown, DE
10 June 2016